TREACHERY
at Martinique Isle

DAUGHTERS OF THE HIGH SEAS
BOOK 1

TREACHERY
at Martinique Isle

RACHEL CHERÍE

Book design copyright © 2011 *Cover design by Shawn Collins*
Interior design by April Marciszewski

Published in the United States of America

ISBN: 978-0-99988-180-4
1. Fiction: Sea Stories
2. Juvenile Fiction: Action & Adventure: Pirates
11.08.22

Dedicated to:

The real Alex
and all the good times
we had together.

Love always,

Jacq

Prologue

"Run!

"As the word rang out, every soul in the inn scattered. Men snagged jugs of liquor off of the counter when the tenders weren't looking, and women gathered their children in the folds of their dresses and ran up the large stairwell off to one side of the room.

"Screams, whistles, and harsh laughter could be heard approaching the doors of the highly-esteemed inn. It was then, when the hopes of all those hidden behind counters and barred doors began to fade, that the innkeeper bravely walked to the front, dragging an old cannon behind him. He opened the lower door, used by his dog, and poked the nose of the cannon through it. The lubbers outside laughed—until he lit it."

"And then it shot off and knocked all the sea lubbers dead, right?" a girl's voice interrupted as the parrot on her shoulder squawked approval.

"Well," the man continued, chuckling, "they say that they all fell dead, but I don't believe it!"

She gasped. "You don't?"

"No! I believe that a few of them escaped the cannon ball, and shall come back when he least expects it. They want his gold—all of it. They shall arrive in a group, and

they shall circle him, and, seeing how he was once a pirate, they shall try and cut out his sin-stained heart."

"Oh! How awful!" The parrot whistled as her hand covered her mouth.

"Yes, m'dear. How awful." He chuckled, putting his arm around the small girl's shoulders. "But, the truly awful part is that they shall not find a heart in this man."

"Oh! Why not? What did he do with it?"

"He either gave it away or buried it with his treasure. Which do you think?" he returned, smiling.

The girl smiled sheepishly. "If he had a little girl, I bet he would give it to her," she replied sincerely, tucking her hands into the deep pockets of her trousers.

The man smiled and patted her bandana-topped, strawberry-blond head. His eyes misted over as he looked into her big, hazel pools. "No matter what happens," he said, kneeling to look her right in the eye, "promise me that wherever you go—you shall always be who you are."

The girl stared at him for a moment. "Of course, Captain Taylor, but what do you mean?"

Scooping her into his arms, he walked to the ship's railing, and together, they stared out to the sea, vast and endless, without flaw or thought. "I'm just saying, Jacq. Just saying." He sighed.

The two were silent for a moment before Jacq broke it, saying, "Captain Taylor! What be the name of this here port we be sailin' toward?" Her eyes glinted while her parrot gurgled on her shoulder in the misty air.

Smiling gratefully at her efforts to cheer him, he pointed as he set her down, explaining, "That, little lass, be the harbor of *Port de Couler de Bateaux*."

"French?" She snorted, snapping into a standing position, causing the parrot to screech.

"Aye, a French name, but not a French port." Looking at the bird, he chuckled. "You needn't worry, Bill. The French were here many years ago, but haven't set foot here in ages. I personally think it was named to mock them," he explained.

"Oh," she said in surprise, looking over the parrot at the man. "What's it mean?"

He grinned. "It be Port of Sinking Ships, lass."

"Maybe," she responded, eyeing the mass in the distance, "there's a reason the French haven't been back. It doesn't sound like it's worth its salt to dock our ship."

"Perhaps." The captain laughed. "But we'll be gone before too long. Just make sure your language be fittin' for a lady such as yerself! Speak as if your mother were here!"

"Aye, aye, Captain!" she declared, smiling as broadly as possible.

As quick as the winds would take them, they arrived at their destination and docked the ship in the harbor. From there, having landed in the dark of night, Captain Taylor and Jacq left the crew and, hand in hand, made their way to an inn called Midway Zebra that sat nestled in the back corner of the town's square. The girl, who had just recently passed her tenth birthday, stared up at the large zebra head that stretched out from the wall above the door of the inn. "Captain, is that really a zebra?" Dropping his hand, she pointed up, tilting her head to one side. "Where are they from?"

"Yes, Jacq." He laughed. "Zebras look like that, and they are from the continent of Africa, way down south of here."

"I wish to see one, one day." She sighed, staring up at the sign and letting her hand fall to her side. "Do you think I shall?"

"Perhaps. You never know where you shall be tomorrow until you get there. Remember that always." Reaching down, he took her small hand in his as they entered the inn.

Just down the street, being chauffeured to the very same inn, sat a girl the exact age of Jacq, with long, brilliant hair of an identical shade. She sat, clad in a lovely, pink-colored dress, beside a tall, lovely but pale woman known to many as Madam Thorpe. Her husband was a merchant, fat and full of goods and money. One of the highest ranking in her social class, Madam Priscilla Thorpe was rarely seen by the commoner. However, her husband was away on business, and she was ill in a strange town. Upon arriving at Midway Zebra, she finally spoke. "Thank you, Homer. Let us out here." Then, she held out her gloved hand to the girl, who had slid out of the carriage and opened her hand for the lady. "Thank you, Alexandria." Tipping Homer, the lady then turned to the inn, straightened her long green skirts, and glided forward with a hint of exhaustion in her step.

Inside the inn, the tall woman picked her way to the counter and requested in her smooth, elegant voice, "I need a room and cannot look for another inn this night."

The older woman who turned to look at her sneered, a gold tooth gleaming in her mouth. "Did ya be wantin' to be lookin' fer another one, miss?"

Madam Thorpe stared at her a moment, turning even whiter than she was. "Nay, ma'am," she muttered, short of

tightly to each other. However, Madam Thorpe was getting weaker by the moment, and her grasp began to fade.

Alexandria's overcast eyes sought the innkeeper. "We must take her to her room now; she is quite ill."

"Of course, child," the woman agreed. Hoisting Madam Thorpe up onto her shoulders, the innkeeper carried her to the stairs and on up to her room. Taking a deep breath, Alexandria glanced around the common room full of noisy men, women, and children. Their conversation was little more to her than a din, mumbling in her ears. She swallowed a lump in her throat and, hoping Madam Thorpe would get better soon, she wrung her fingers and took off up the stairs after the two women, oblivious to the scene playing out at the bar.

Captain Taylor knelt in front of Jacq, who was holding Bill tightly to herself. His eyes brimming with tears, he choked, "Jacq, you are a special girl. You're the only one that I can travel the world with, but I'm going to ask you to do something for me, lass. You can say yes, or you can say no."

The girl, saying nothing, stared at him with her big eyes.

"I need to know," he paused, searching her face, "if I can leave you here for a little while, with Fred."

"Because you need the money?" she asked, understanding more than he wished her to.

"Aye, Jacq."

Shifting her weight back and forth between her feet, she continued to gaze deep into the captain's eyes. "Shall you come back for me?"

"As soon as I can." He could feel the hot tears pricking at the backs of his eyes, begging to be released onto his face. Determinedly, he blinked them away.

She eyed Fred for a moment, who smiled kindly at her. Leaning forward, she whispered, "Has Fred been to Africa?"

Captain Taylor chuckled a little, the tears almost pouring from his eyes. "Aye, he has been to Africa."

Her eyes grew larger yet. "Has he seen zebras?"

"You know, I think maybe he has."

Her eyes sparkled in the dim, smoky light. A small smile that was far beyond her age blossomed on her face. "Aye, Captain. I shall stay here and wait for you. Then, when you come back for me, we can go to Africa together and see the zebras." She stood content with this arrangement a moment, but then, her smile fading, she held out Bill.

"Nay, Jacq." His hand was heavy as he touched his palm to her cheek. "You take care of Bill. He likes you more than he likes me anyway." Resting a hand on each of her tiny shoulders, he forced a small but sincerely proud smile. "Your mother would be so proud of you."

Throwing her arms about the broad-shouldered, heavy-hearted sea captain, causing Bill to squawk irritably, the girl whispered, "Come back soon, Cap'n."

After releasing her, he rose and looked at Fred. Coughing a little, Fred sputtered, "Just a moment, matey. I seem to have gotten a pinch of sand in me eye."

Pointing a long finger at him, Captain Taylor commanded, "Keep her safe."

The innkeeper, putting the money in the captain's hand and shaking it, replied, "Fear ye not, good Cap'n. No harm

shall come to even a hair of this child's head." The captain looked a little skeptical, but Fred straightened indignantly and spat, "Frederick Bumbleridge is a man of his word. There ain't no better man to trust in this here port."

With that, the captain and the girl saluted each other, and he departed swiftly, knowing that if he stayed and thought about it, he would change his mind.

Jacq stood in the middle of the floor, staring after him for a few minutes. She was waiting for him to come back and get her even though deep, deep down she knew better. She so wanted to see the zebras of Africa. Yet, the longer she stood there, the more she accepted that the good Captain Taylor would not be returning to get her that day ... or the next. Within minutes of his leaving, rain started to fall from the sky. The girl that he'd left behind wandered to the nearest window and stared out into the cobblestone street, watching the raindrops splash into puddles. After a few moments, looking curiously at the parrot, she whispered, "It's the truth then. It rains when we're sad."

Clearing his throat, Fred Bumbleridge put his hand on the girl's shoulder. She diverted her gaze from beyond the window to his face. "Now then, come, child," he requested, holding his hand out to her. "There be someone else I be wantin' ya to meet."

"Be there a Mrs. Bumbleridge, sir?" she inquired, mimicking his manner of speech.

"Haha!" he laughed heartily, kneeling to look her in the eye. "There be, miss! And, I beseech ye, pray tell an old man, what be the name of that there parrot o'yarn?"

The parrot turned its head to one side and winked at the older man. "His name is Big Beak Bill, but we just call him Bill for short. He's a blue-throated macaw from the west." Her eyes twinkling, she queried, "Have you ever been to the west?"

A wry smile creased the innkeeper's lips. "Aye, lass. And if I were still atop the seven seas, I would be a mite inclined to take ye to see the zebras of Africa meself."

She smiled then, delighted that he would say such a lovely thing to her. Holding out his hand, he waited as she tucked the blue and yellow bird under her arm before sliding her hand into his. Together, they walked into the back of the inn to the kitchen. "Jemima!" he bellowed upon entering the room. "I have a beautiful present for ye, me lass."

"Be that so, Fred?" asked a woman, who Jacq saw peep out above a barrel.

"It be," he replied, swelling with pride over his perfect find.

"Be it luck, then, that I be havin' a present for ye as well!" she chimed. Not seeing the child and bird that stood by her husband's side, she twirled a pink dress out onto the floor. Flapping his wings, Bill screeched in protest at the blur of color. Jacq stared wide-eyed at the girl that appeared in front of her.

"By the powers!" the innkeepers gasped in unison. They glanced back and forth between the girls as the two stared at each other. Alexandria thought her head was still spinning, though she'd stopped twirling. There, staring her right in the face, was her very own self, but with no style!

Both girls turned to their purchaser, blurting, "Who is she?" as they pointed at each other.

"What powers be at work in our house tonight?" Frederick asked his wife suspiciously. "How be it that twins as these do not recognize each other?"

Jemima shrugged. "Perhaps it be known in higher places that we be needin' more help aboot this place." She pushed Alexandria toward Jacq. "Introduce yerself like a proper young lady, now."

Of course, Alexandria, being a proper young lady, did a small curtsey. "I am Alexandria Luray Thorpe. And you are?"

Jacq looked the girl over, then, seeing as she was wearing trousers, a blouse, and a bandana, simply bowed in return. "I have one of those long names too. Jacqueline Luray Taylor, but you can call me Jacq." After an awkward moment of silence, she asked, "Can I call you Alex?"

Alexandria stared at her. *Alex? The name of a lad?* Not even the proper name of a lad! But then, what kind of a name was Jacq for a young lady?

"I suppose that you calling me Alex shall be acceptable," she replied, her voice sounding higher than she wished it to.

"Good!" Crossing her arms and pulling her bottom lip between her teeth, Jacq looked this new acquaintance up and down a brief moment. "So, Alex, do you wash dishes?" she asked, raising an eyebrow. "Because I'd much rather swab the floors."

Chapter
1

"Jacq!"

A young woman, her hair in a braid that hung just past her shoulder blades and her head covered by a bandana, stood gazing out toward the sea. The smell of the sea barely attainable to her senses as a gentle breeze blew it in, causing her loose blouse to billow about her slender frame. At the sound of the name being hollered, she closed her eyes and then glanced down at the roof she was standing on. Then, taking one more look at the vast ocean, she walked to a flagstaff next to the roof and, throwing her trouser-clad legs around it, slid all the way down to the ground. Hearing the jingle of the coins she had attached to the sash about her waist, she stopped to admire them at the bottom of the flagstaff.

"Jacq!" a hoarse whisper interrupted her thoughts.

Turning, she came face to face with the large blue eyes of a young man who, being taller than she, was as lanky as the pole she'd just slid down. "Miata!" she growled between her teeth. "You know Alex gets awfully upset

when you come around. She still believes that you are the reason that she was left here."

"Aye, Jacq, me mate, but that were nigh on eight years ago, and I had been needin' that money." He twisted the corner of his rough gray sweater around his fingers. "And I be needin' to speak with ye aboot some pressin' matters."

Folding her arms, Jacq sighed. "What is it, Miata?"

He leaned casually against the building, his fingers still busily worrying the corner of his sweater. "Well, mate, it's aboot this mate o' mine. Ya see, I be thinkin' that he be turnin' me in shortly."

Her eyebrow rising, she tightened her arms over her stomach. "What would cause you to believe such a thing?"

"Well," the young man began in a soft tone, locking her eye contact, "I know that he be low on cash nowadays, and I overheard a conversation he was havin' with a mate o' his."

"You were eavesdropping again?" Jacq questioned, shoving her hands into her pockets.

Miata's face turned pink. "I overheard him talking to another fellow aboot some sort o' a plan that they was to be hatchin' together."

Jacq's eyebrow shot up at this. "That's all nonsense, Miata. What could they possibly have been talking about that would concern a fellow like you unless you were going to help them?"

"Well, they started off with some flimflammer about the sea and a ship, and then one o' 'em, I'm not sure which, started blatherin' aboot kickin' one o' their mates out. Then they went on aboot this lass that they'd been wantin' to find." The corner of Jacq's mouth turned up in a look

of disbelief. Miata leaned closer to her and whispered, "I think me mate wants to get rid of me so that he can court me sister."

"Miata..." Jacq shook her head in amusement. "You do not even have a sister."

The young man blinked. "I do so! Well, I mean, I might be havin' one..."

She shook her head in disbelief now.

"Jacq..."

"Miata, you're paranoid." She chuckled. Then, hearing her name called again, she smiled and retorted, "You do not have a sister. And, even if you had a sister, I wouldn't be worryin' about anyone trying to court her. Nobody knows she exists." She patted him on the shoulder and headed toward the side door to the inn.

Hurrying inside, Jacq all but ran into a girl clothed in a mauve-colored skirt that hid her feet, a cream-colored blouse, and a beige vest that laced up the front, like Jacq's shirt. The two were still the same height and could easily be mistaken for each other. Their biggest differences now were the biggest differences they'd had the night they first met—their styles. Her eyes narrowing slightly, the girl in the dress tilted her head.

"Whom were you speaking to?"

Jacq smiled. "Nobody you would wish to speak with, Alex," she assured her. "Was Jemima calling for me?"

"Aye." She narrowed her eyes as Jacq brushed past her. "It was not that thief, was it?"

Jacq was already too far away from Alex to hear her question and was twirling about as she headed toward the kitchen, humming the tune of the same song she'd been

humming the night the inn became her new home. As she passed through the dining area, she waved at everyone she knew, which made up of the majority of the crowd. Her parrot, Bill, swooped down from a ledge and landed on her shoulder. "Just think, Bill. That sign is the closest that we ever came to seeing a zebra." Bill tilted his head to one side and blinked. "I don't know," she responded glumly. "I just don't know."

Swinging the door to the kitchen open, she sighed heavily.

"Jacq! Jacq, get down here, by thunder!" Jemima Bumbleridge hollered out the window at the top of her lungs. Smiling, Jacq reached over and tapped her on the shoulder. Whirling around, the woman gasped. "Careful, lass! There be many strange powers at work these days."

Startled, Jacq inquired, "What powers, Mrs. Bumbleridge?"

Jemima, who had aged rather rapidly since the girls arrived eight years earlier, laid a frail hand on the young woman's cheek. "There be much aboot, Jacq. Fred be wantin' to see ye."

Leaving Bill on her shoulder, Jacq sprinted upstairs to the room of Frederick Bumbleridge. She had hardly knocked when he called her in, knowing already that it was her. Opening the door, she found him sitting on the edge of the Bumbleridge's large bed. His silvering beard slumped on his thin chest as he stared out the small window across from him. Quietly, she sat at his feet, legs crossed, and waited. Shifting his eyes to her, he smiled and ran his fingertips along Bill's back. Jacq thought that his eyes looked more watery than usual, and his hands

shook more than they ever had before. "Jacq," he finally managed to mumble, "yer services here, fer me wife an' me, be more than anythin' else ye could give us. Me days be numbered, lass."

"Everyone's days are numbered," Jacq returned, searching his eyes for some kind of explanation. Out of the corner of her eye, she saw a crumpled piece of paper on his pillow.

"Of that, ye be right, Jacq." He leaned forward to talk to her, just as Captain Taylor had done eight years prior. "But me days be more numbered than yers." The corner of her mouth lifted slightly as he smiled at her. "Now, I be wantin' ye to keep this here locket safe for me," he continued after a pause. Jacq started to open her mouth in protest, but he held up his hand, and she said nothing. "Ye be the closest thing that I be havin' to a daughter, and fer that reason, I be wantin' it to be yarn now." He slipped the gold chain and locket he'd produced from his pocket around her neck.

"What is inside?" she asked, taking the oddly shaped, golden charm in her palm to examine it more closely. It shone beautifully in the light.

"It be a riddle, child. The most clever trail to riches ye could ever ask fer." Her brow creased at his answer. Laying his hand on her cheek, he whispered, "Be not worryin' aboot it right now, lass. Ye will understand when the time is proper." Jacq smiled at him and nodded. Sitting back and smiling peacefully, he added, "Off with ye now, Jacq. I'd hate to be keepin' ye from yer chores."

Springing to her feet, she straightened her knee-high boots and walked slowly toward the door. As she reached for the door handle, Fred called out, "And Jacq…" She

turned to look at him. "I be wantin' to apologize fer somethin'." Her brow furrowing again, she turned to face him. "I'm sorry I couldn't take ye to see the zebras of Africa."

She smiled, her eyes moistening slightly. "You have done much more for me than taking me to see the zebras ever would have done." She sighed, remembering the sad eyes of Captain Taylor before he'd forced himself to walk out the door. Fred smiled back at her, then laid back and closed his eyes. Swallowing an iron lump in her throat, Jacq walked out the door and down the upper hall to the window at the east end at the top of the stairwell. As she held still, looking out into the late afternoon, she noticed some gray clouds overhead. The sky darkened and then it started to rain. A heavy chill settled over her countenance and an eerie feeling slithered through her veins as the memory of her last night in the presence of Captain Taylor replayed in her mind so vividly it was as if she was watching it reenact outside the window in the cobblestone square.

As Jacq stood staring out the window, Bill tilted his head to look at her. "What times are these, dear Bill?" she asked in a low tone, her gaze moving to the parrot.

"These are strange times at the Midway Zebra." Pivoting about, Jacq found herself face to face with her twin, who was holding a small monkey, Jemima's pet. Around her throat hung a chain. Dangling at the end was a nearly identical charm to the one Fred had given Jacq. "Madam Bumbleridge has given me charge of Frankincense."

Jacq turned so Alex could see her locket, then dropped it into her blouse. "Aye. I cannot make any sense of it—"

A low *kaboom!* sounded at the end of her sentence, as if punctuating her statement. A shiver went through the inn, and, all feeling it, everyone began to look about for the source of the distant noise. Both girls' brows wrinkling in confusion, Jacq looked to Alex and asked with forced seriousness, "Are you cooking?"

"No!" At the end of her retort, there came a loud *kawack!* The inn shook violently, threatening to collapse as if some blow had been rendered to it. Grabbing the railing to prevent themselves from falling, the two girls stared at each other in shock. Splintered wood hissed through the air, landing on tables down below. Shrieks and curses flew from the mouths of customers. The two girls turned to find that the front of the inn was ablaze. Running past her sister, Alex fled down the stairs; Jacq slid down the banister as Bill flew above her.

"Ahoy!" she yelled as she hit the floor on one knee, one foot, and one hand in a tripod position. The crowd turned to look at her as she bounced to her feet. She suddenly envisioned all of the people in the room staring at her as sheep. Their eyes were empty, bewildered, and wild. Though they bunched together, an overtone of skittishness suggested they would scatter at any moment. Hardly anything could be heard over the din, which had left everyone's ears ringing. Nobody moved. They were all stuck to the floor, huddled together, by an odorless presence in the room—stark fear.

Closing her eyes and shaking her head to rid herself of the sheep vision, she called out, "This way!" and bounded toward the back of the inn. Quick footsteps thundered across the floor as the people uncertainly ran after the girl.

Coming up behind them, Alex, still carrying the monkey, called for them to follow Jacq to the east side door, where she would lead them out onto the streets.

Crying women, holding their children closely to their bosoms, filed out first, followed by men, several of who were limping noticeably. Alex, gray and severely red-eyed from the smoke, reached Jacq's side, peeling Frankincense off her waist and ushering him out the door. "That is everyone, Jacq. There are none else who are able to leave. All the others shall not move with any persuasion—killed by the flying debris or the explosion."

Rubbing her eyes, burning from the heat and smoke with the back of her sleeve, Jacq nodded. "Then we must go back for the Bumbleridges!"

Taking her sister's hand, Alex turned to hurry back to the dining area. Bent to try to avoid too much of the billowing, black cloud, they did not notice the two figures in the middle of the eating hall until they had already hopped the counter. They were actually rather surprised to see the aging couple standing, facing the north door, each with a bag. "Come!" the girls called out, gesturing toward the east-side door as they choked on the smoke. "Leave now! We shall gather our things and follow!"

In unison, the couple turned. Amidst the blaze, they suddenly seemed twenty years younger. Jemima, having two pistols tucked into the sash about her waist and a rapier at her side with a gallant, flowing skirt about her, looked as if she had just stepped out of a book. Fred, with two rapiers dangling from his waistline, smiled devilishly, his black necktie never looking quite as bold as it did right then when he was standing in front of an orange flame.

"We've packed fer ye," Frederick Bumbleridge replied slowly. Jemima smiled, her gold tooth sparkling fiercely in the firelight. Tossing Jacq and Alex the bags, the elderly couple bowed and made their way toward the stairs. "Now, off with ye, afore yer time fer escapin' gets away from ye." Looking Jacq right in the eye from across the room, he hollered, "Run!"

Opening and closing their mouths several times, the girls stared as they watched the two ascend the stairwell. Alex was the first to come to her senses. Taking Jacq by the arm, she dragged her twin toward the east door. Jacq had finally consented to go, grabbing up her frantic parrot and releasing him out the door, when a loud *whack* from within caught their attention; they had to look. Through the climbing smoke and flame, they watched a dark figure enter into the once warm and homey dining area of the Midway Zebra. Flailing his sword, which reflected the jumping flames all too well, the sinister man bellowed, "Black Fred! Gold Jem! We're back! We knows yer in here, we do!" He stumbled about, allowing his eyes to rove the room wildly as if he expected to find some hidden clue.

Jacq's eyes glittered. "It's just as Captain Taylor said!" she whispered excitedly. "It is just as he said! These are pirates…"

"Pirates? Captain Taylor told you stories of such things as these? How did you sleep at night?" Alex gasped as she stepped out into the rain of the darkening night, coughing fitfully. Howling angrily, Frankincense took hold of Alex's hand tightly with his, baring his teeth in outrage of being left outside alone.

Jacq threw a glare at her before she went back to staring into the room. One of the pirates saw them peeking in. "Ahoy! There be more than two old pirates in this inn!"

Darting out of the doorway, Jacq snatched her sister by the wrist and stumbled down the wet cobblestone alley. Her chest hurt horribly from the amount of smoke she had breathed in, and it took all she had to continue racing away from the inn. Once they could no longer hear the inn burning or see its flames reaching toward the sky, they collapsed onto the street. Rain fell steadily now, and the girls coughed loud enough Alex was afraid they would wake the dead. Tears streamed down their dirty faces. Their eyes were hot and itched with a ferocity Jacq was afraid she would never get rid of. Between coughs and gasps of air, Alex whimpered, "Where do we go now?"

"Be ye in need of somewhere to go, lass?" a young man's voice questioned.

Both girls turned and inhaled sharply, making them cough all the harder. "Miata!" Jacq coughed. "This night is not a good night to be scaring Alex and me!"

The big grin on his face faded, especially after he caught a glimpse of Alex's glare. "I be merely tryin' to help me mates, Jacq." His brow furrowed as he took in their bedraggled appearance. Bill floated down and landed on Jacq's shoulder.

Ignoring Alex's nonverbal protest, Jacq agreed, and the two followed Miata into the darkening, wet streets of town as the Midway Zebra burned steadily to the ground behind them.

Chapter
2

Jacq's eyes flew open. Sitting up quickly, she scanned the room, wishing the night before had been just a dream. However, just as she recalled, Alex and Frankincense lay nearby, nestled amongst some hay; Bill was roosting on a ledge not far off; smoke was still rising away to the northwest where the Midway Zebra once stood; and Miata was squatting not too far off, with a warm fire and something that smelled like eggs sizzling in a pan over it. Dusting the hay off of herself, she grabbed her bag, which she'd been using as a pillow, and dragged it with her to the fire. The morning air was warm with late spring sunshine, but she still had a chill deep inside of her.

Within seconds of her waking, Alex was following her to the fire. She eyed Miata's eggs and then questioned, "Should I ask where you obtained those?"

"Does it matter?"

"Of course it does!" Alex retorted. "I will not be one to eat stolen eggs."

Jacq rolled her eyes and sat back on her heels. Miata's face lit up with a warm, bright smirk that anyone except Alex would have smiled back to. "Well, lass, ye steal yer eggs every morn."

Alex gasped. "How dare you! I do not! We get them from our own chickens!"

Jacq winced and sighed.

Shifting his weight excitedly, he returned, "Be ye askin' yer hens fer their eggs every morn?"

Alex shut her mouth, and her eyes narrowed.

"If not, lass, then ye be stealin'. An' if ye do, an' those hens don't be sayin' aye, and ye be takin' 'em anyway, then ye be stealin' even more!" He straightened his face in an attempt to be convincing, obviously having used this argument before.

Her nostrils flaring, Alex glanced down at Jacq. Her mouth turning up at the corner in a smile, Jacq simply shrugged and eyed the eggs. "Fine," Alex growled, flopping down beside her sister. "I shall eat one egg, but no more."

Miata, maintaining a controlled, amiable composure, handed them each a wooden plate and a knife to eat their eggs. As he dished them up one egg each, Jacq cleared her throat, which was still raw. "We should look and see what the Bumbleridges gave us."

Alex nodded. "Yes. We need to know if there are any legal matters that need attending to."

Shoving her egg into her mouth, Jacq reached for her bag and began to dig through the surprisingly dry contents. After the storm the night before, she was sure everything would be soaked. Jacq mentally shrugged. *The canvas must be waterproof.* Beneath a change of clothes

and a cloak was a letter. They each had a personalized copy of a very similar note. Alex's read:

Dear Alexandria,

Unlucky times have befallen Frederick and I. We'll be leaving all our things to ye and yer sister, Jacqueline, may the good LORD bless both yer souls. Ye both be having a locket from us, ye with the second half, and she with the first. We have attended to all our debts and legal matters, and leave none behind for ye to pay or be reconciled with. Our inn be both of yers after our deaths. Take these Fred and I have packed for ye with ye at all times, lass. And as ye go looking for yer past, be most careful not to stray too far from yer future.

May the good LORD keep yer souls and bless ye always. And please, be a dear and take care of Frankincense.

Jemima

Sitting back, Jacq stared at her locket for a few moments, then remained in deep thought for nigh on a quarter of an hour. Occasionally she would glance at either Alex or Miata, who were watching her earnestly, but then resume her position. Finally, she sighed, suggesting, "Perhaps we should look at what else is in the bags?"

Nodding, the two plunged their hands into their respective bags. Feeling a cold, round object greet her fingertips, Jacq withdrew her hand, holding a beautiful compass obviously made for her. *They knew they were going to die*, she thought, coughing at this idea. Tears from the night before requested to be set free, but she suppressed them.

When Alex pulled out a compass as well, Jacq nodded, and they continued their search. Pulling out a bag about a quarter the size of the one through which they were digging, Alex cautiously opened it to find that it held three even smaller satchels. Jacq watched as she opened the first one and revealed money. Alex's eyes sparkled.

Smiling, Jacq yanked her bag of the same size out of the way and thrust her hand back inside. At this, Jacq's heart skipped a beat. She could feel a carved handle and a smooth, metal—barrel? *No!* Pulling the bag onto her lap, she peered into the opening, afraid of what would greet her. Her breath escaped. Alex, who'd been ogling over the money, looked up when she heard her sister struggling for breath. Miata began to fidget again as he watched Jacq slowly put her hand into the bag again. Smiling sheepishly, she slowly pulled out a firearm.

"What a strange gift to give you." Alex laughed, hoping it would help Jacq relax. Reaching into her bag, the same metallic coldness greeted her fingertips. She paled.

Jacq swallowed. "And we're supposed to carry these everywhere we go?"

Alex's eyes widened and brimmed with tears. Jacq watched as she burst into a thousand water droplets, all landing in a sobbing puddle of sorrow. "What is happening to us?"

"Nothing yet's the thing," Miata said, trying to be consoling. Jacq smiled at him, her face gentle and acknowledging his efforts. Grinning sheepishly and standing to stretch, he walked to the window of the loft he'd snuck them into the night before.

Turning back to Alex, Jacq sighed. "We've got to find answers," she said, speaking in a soft tone.

"They gave us bullets and gun powder!" Alex whimpered, wrapping the other two little bags up together and shoving them into the bag with the gun.

"A lot?"

Alex nodded.

"Great." Jacq toyed with the locket for several seconds before she suddenly stopped short and whispered, "Alex! Give me your locket!"

Dabbing her eyes with the corner of her skirt, Alex fumbled to slip off the chain and hand it to Jacq. "Why?"

"Because," Jacq said, holding the two lockets in the air side by side, "they form a heart!" Jacq laughed loudly, waking Bill, who squawked and flapped his wings in annoyance at her outburst. Frankincense opened his eyes and chirped at Alex from where she'd left him. Vaulting to her feet, Jacq twirled about.

"And the significance of that, Jacq, is what?"

Jacq, her eyes wide with wonder, dropped down beside Alex.

"Oh no." Alex laughed, holding up her hand. "Do not tell me. It is a treasure map or some such nonsense. Captain Taylor sure did a splendid job of filling your head with ridiculous stories. Striped horses, treasure maps, lands far to the west, flight, furry creatures with the bills of ducks." Alex stared piteously at her sister. "I do not know any other soul so full of nonsense."

Like a young child with his or her first new toy, Jacq ignored Alex's spiteful remarks. She did not even hear the bitter words her twin had spoken, let alone take them to

heart. Handing Alex her locket back and leaping again to her feet, Jacq urged, "Open it! Open it!" Fumbling with the clasp on hers, Jacq found her excitement was so near the point of uncontainable that she could hardly command her fingers to do her bidding. Once she had popped the tiny treasure open, she saw these words inscribed onto the soft metal: *At the SW sea, turn your back, to the inn / lies the key, Across the way.*

"Oh! What's it say in yours, Alex?"

Though it was against everything in her practical mind, Alex found she was rather curious now. Opening her locket, she read, "Stay and it will lead ye, True to the marker / to set the treasure free, At last to dig in sand." She sighed after a moment of silence. "Why did I get the one that hardly makes any sense?"

"Maybe," Jacq, wide-eyed and still dancing with excitement, sputtered, "maybe it's just scrambled—a puzzle."

"Say," Miata spoke up. Talk of money always peaked his interest, and buried treasure sounded fascinating. "I might be havin' a mate that might be able to aid us."

"You do?" Jacq cried, clutching the locket to her chest.

"*Us?*" Alex said in disbelief.

Miata crossed his arms. "If ye be enlisting the help of me mate, then ye be takin' me with ye on yer treasure hunt!"

Jacq turned big eyes to Alex. Alex, glowering ever so obviously, finally rolled her eyes and threw up her hands. "Very well, very well. But there are two things I do not like about this arrangement."

"What be those?" Miata asked, seating himself in front of them, all but shaking with excitement.

"First off, I dislike leaving the matters of the Bumbleridges so suddenly, and for the second, we do not know anything about this mate of his," she challenged, shoving all of her things back into her bag with a force that made Frankincense jump.

"Well," Jacq responded, stuffing her things energetically into her bag and then holding her hand out for Bill, who immediately came to his master, "the letter did say that all of the legal matters and such are tended to and paid for. They left us no strings, and we can begin to piece together who we are on the way! You shall see that it shall all come together as we go. As for Miata's mate, he can tell us about him."

Smiling a dazzling smile, Jacq turned convincingly to Miata, hoping that his friend was not in the same department of work as he.

"Well … ye see … Me mate is a tad different from most folks ye ever met afore, I imagine." The girls both stopped what they were doing and leaned closer to the thief. Jacq raised her eyebrow questioningly. "It's just that …" Miata sighed. And then he squirmed. His smile turned to an uncomfortable grimace. "He just …" Miata sat and stared at them for several seconds, then flung himself forward and whispered to them.

Reeling back, the girls, eyes wider than they had ever been before, stared at each other.

About two hours later, the three were standing in front of a rugged yet well kept building. "This could be," Jacq

muttered, "the reason that the French left." Alex nodded in agreement as she stared up at the large sign in the shape of a helmet with horns coming out the sides of it. Thoughtfully, Jacq turned to Miata, who was staring just like Alex. "He really believes he's a descendent from the Vikings?"

Bobbing his head in violent and sincere protest, Bill whistled at the sign.

Nodding, Miata replied, "I'm sorry. I don't think I've ever been here during the day. I have never afore seen that sign."

Glancing at the sign once again, Jacq inhaled slowly, mentally preparing herself for this meeting, and then held her arm out to signal Miata to lead the way. Running his fingers through his loose, jaw-length hair, he escorted them to the front door, knocked, and waited, but no one came. Looking awkwardly back at them, he pushed through the door into a warm room with a huge bear rug on the floor. A fire in a large, open hearth on the opposite wall burned brightly. Relics of old ships hung from the ceiling and leaned against walls in a cacophony of wood and canvas. All the furniture in the room was furry with the hides of creatures, and several different helmets with various ornaments lined the mantel above the fireplace.

Clearing his throat, Miata called out meekly, "Hullo! Geoffrey! It's yer mate, Miata …" All three of them strained their ears to listen for a reply, but none came. Frankincense, seeing Bill preening on Jacq's shoulder, suddenly became interested in the parrot's tail feathers. Releasing Alex's hand, the monkey grabbed for Bill's tail. Squawking irritably at the unwanted attention, Bill

flapped his wings, hopping to the top of Jacq's head for refuge.

"Contain Frank, would you?" Jacq growled. Bill nodded in agreement, squawking down at the creature smiling up at him.

"Who's Frank?" Alex snapped.

Jacq gestured to the mammal, which had moved to one of the furry chairs to get a better view of Bill. "The monkey."

As Alex watched him, he minded, keeping his fingers to himself. She turned to her twin, crossing her arms. "You can't just call him Frank. Jemima named him Frankincense!"

Rolling her eyes, Jacq looked down at the monkey again, who stuck his tongue out at her when Alex wasn't looking. "I bet she called him Frank when nobody else was listening. I called you Alex the first day I met you. What's the difference?"

Frank bared his teeth at Jacq and pushed on a clay pot near the end of the sofa.

"Frank!" she snapped, catching the pot before it hit the ground.

Ever so pleased with himself, he grabbed Jacq around her leg and prepared to climb up to irritate Bill, who was already flapping madly in protest.

"Alex! Control the monkey!" Jacq pleaded, shaking her leg to try to get the beasty off.

Sighing, Alex held out her hand, and the monkey came to her without argument, obediently sliding his hand into hers. "Frank?"

The monkey smiled.

"Very well," she muttered, shaking her head. "Frank."

Jacq grinned, satisfied, as she replaced the pot.

"Somebody called?"

The trio turned to see a man dressed in an expensive and well-tailored outfit, with matching coat, pants, and sash, standing stiffly before them. Jacq took a giant step away from the pot. He directed his attention to her. "I see you were admiring Mr. Pierce's pottery. That is one of his favorites."

Smiling uncomfortably, Jacq glanced sideways at Alex and laughed awkwardly. "Oh? Is that right? Of course it is ... It is lovely ..."

Nodding, the man inquired, "Are you here to see Mr. Pierce?"

"Aye." Miata smiled and bowed. "I'm Geoffrey's mate, Miata, and these are two of me mates, Jacq and Alex."

"Of course, Miata," the man agreed in his stuffy monotone voice. He disappeared for a few moments, then reappeared, saying, "He shall see you now. He is in his recreational room, playing a new game that came to him early this morning while he was practicing his spear toss."

The girls exchanged big-eyed glances. "Wonderful," Miata mumbled, rolling his eyes.

Escorting them to the recreational room, the man gestured toward a young man, whom the girls assessed to be Geoffrey Pierce, donning a fuzzy pair of goatskin pants and a dark pair of knee-high boots. His light, messy hair reflected a rugged flare that was contradictory to the educated calm of his eyes—despite their boyish gleam. Other than his athletically muscular arms, his physique wasn't much to speak of being pale and average, giving away the fact that he'd spent more time reading than exercising.

He was positioned opposite of a large target painted to cover most of the wall. As the visiting group of three entered, Pierce launched a small spear into the center of the target where it joined three other small spears that were already lodged in the wall. As it stuck, he clapped his hands and laughed in pleasure at his success. "Ha! Did you see that, Mister Bibbs? Four in a row! My best score yet!"

"What be ye aboot, Geoffrey?" Miata called out, scratching the side of his head.

"Miata!" Pierce whirled about to face him, a jovial expression splitting his face. "I've invented a new game!"

"Aye, Geoffrey, I can see that. What be the name and object of this here game o' yarn?"

"I think I shall be namin' this one 'spears.' Someday, in the future, they'll be throwin' these miniature spears into a target and thinkin' o' me," he gloated.

Miata smiled uneasily at his misguided foresight and waited for him to rejoin them in the present.

After a few brief seconds, he turned his attention back to Miata. "So! What have ya come to see ol' Geoffrey Pierce about?" he asked, his voice sounding fine and proper, though his speech was not. He grinned at Miata, but upon sighting the girls, his back straightened, his small beard bristled, his chest puffed out, and his arms flexed slightly. This combination of his stiff and decorous but rough and macho posturing reminded one of a proper English Viking—if such a thing were ever to exist.

"We be in need of assistance," Miata admitted. Jacq smiled when the thief spoke, for the first time realizing he had a relatively deep voice, at least compared to his friend.

"We be needin' ye to translate somethin' fer us. Would ye be of a mind to do so?"

Looking over Jacq and Alex for a moment, his eyes still glowing like the sun, he grinned and chuckled with glee that Miata had brought them to him. "Of course, matey! What be ya needin' translated?" Jacq and Alex both held up their open lockets. Geoffrey's eyes glistened. "What be this?"

"It's a riddle," Jacq blurted, leaning forward in excitement.

"It was given to us just before the owners died!"

Jacq turned in surprise at the level of enthusiasm in her twin's voice.

"And we be wantin' to know what it means," Miata jumped in.

"Naturally! And that is why ya came here to the master!" He brazenly gestured to himself. "But, we must strike a bargain afore I agree to translate for ya…"

The girls traded wary glances.

"I get to help find whatever it is that it's talkin' about, whether I get any of the spoils or not, agreed?"

Unable to think of any reason—other than they found his seeming obsessions a little unsettling—why not, Jacq shrugged, as did Alex. Miata watched them, unconsciously twisting his fingers in anticipation of their verdict. Hesitantly, Jacq nodded, and the three chimed, "Agreed."

"Wonderful!" he sang out. "Gather our things!" he called to his butler. "I must look at these lockets to determine where we're going!" Motioning for the trio to follow him, he scooped up his loose, puffy shirt and, putting it on, led them to his study.

There, Jacq stared at the walls for only a few brief seconds before realizing that he was completely obsessed. *I touched that pot of his!* She gulped, slightly worried his mental instability might wear off on her. *What are the chances this daft sap can even figure the riddle out?*

Alex, though fascinated at first by the beauty of the drawings of the Viking ships, was soon as disturbed with his obsession as her sister. *She was right*, Alex thought to herself. *This is why the French left.*

Geoffrey hustled about, gathering a few items and papers, a map, and a pen. Once he came to a stop behind his desk, he cleared his throat, getting their attention, and held out his hand. "May I?"

Hesitantly they took off their charm necklaces and handed them over. Miata, who had settled into a hairy chair by the fire, smiled at them as though there was nothing peculiar about this man whatsoever.

"Be careful," Jacq heard herself warn in the quiet air of his office. "These were given to us just yesterday."

Nodding, Geoffrey put on his monocle, making his eye look at least half again its usual size. Smiling at them, he looked over the lockets for a few seconds, then explained, "I can see excellent far away, but when it comes to studying things, I be needin' this. I cannot see anything closer to me than something about me arm's length away. It really hurts me heart that I have such trouble doing what I love so much."

Alex looked at the pictures. "Then who drew all of your beautiful boats?"

"Ah." Geoffrey Pierce smiled proudly. "That would be me scurvy butler. Ya met him. Mr. Bibbs? He's stuffy, usually not much for conversation, but a wonderful artist."

Jacq turned a curled-lip expression toward Alex. Shrugging, Alex shook her head. Taking another deep breath to keep herself calm, Jacq questioned, "So, what do you think of our lockets?"

"They are definitely unique, original, and beautiful," he announced, bobbing his head up and down in approval.

Jacq closed her eyes and rubbed them. "By the powers," she muttered. "Has he even opened the lockets?"

Putting her hand on Jacq's shoulder, Alex turned a woeful expression on her sister. "We gave them to him open."

"Oh!" he burst suddenly. "The engraving! Ya did not tell me there was an engraved message within!"

Alex threw up her hands and turned away from the strange man behind the desk. Jacq, forcing a smile, replied through her teeth, "Aye. The meaning of the message is why we brought them to you. We already knew they were authentic!"

Looking up at them through his eye-enlarging glass, he blinked once and replied simply, "Oh." Then, he hurriedly wrote down the message, glancing rapidly back and forth between the writing and the map sprawled in front of him. After several seconds of intense studying, he burst into loud laughter. "Fools! It is plain as day itself! We are to take a trip across the seas to the other lands. Yo ho, me hearties!" With that, he vaulted to the door, calling for his butler. "Mr. Bibbs! Ready a ship and a captain and a crew! We'll be needin' to sail afore the week is out!"

"Set sail?" Alex verified, whirling about to confront the man, clutching at her throat.

"Set sail to where?" Jacq, though excited about the prospect, felt an undeniable sense of skepticism at his fast conclusion.

"Well," Pierce stammered, seemingly injured they would question him, "to the island of Martinique..." As he spoke, he jammed his finger down on a spot of the map in the Caribbean ocean.

Jacq's brow furrowed. "What makes you so sure?"

"I like to think I'm pretty well informed on how to understand written messages," he said tersely, straightening. His jaw muscles clenched and released at the questioning.

Jacq's brow furrowed further, her lips pursing a little more, and she tapped her fingers on his desk.

"Plus," he added desperately, "legend has it that Francis 'Draque del Mar' Drake landed his ship there nigh on forty years ago and has never been seen or heard from again. Whoever these came from must have sailed with his crew and buried a part of the treasure in secret afore they stole away back to England. The alignment with the coordinates is precise...The other half of the riddle, though, must pertain to the treasure. Half leads to the island, the other half to the treasure itself..."

Shaking her head, Jacq crossed her arms, turning away from Pierce's desk. "This is no good...We can't finance a voyage...Something must be wrong..." Wringing her hands together in thought, she reasoned, *They couldn't have expected us to be able to journey across the sea to get whatever it is they left for us...*

"I can be financin' the voyage!" Pierce piped up, scooting around the corner of his desk and gallantly removing his monocle.

"Why would you do that?" Alex asked, folding her arms in want of an answer.

"Well, it's not every day an opportunity such as this comes across one's path...Sometimes ya got to take a chance..." The girls' faces remained doubtful. "Trust me!" he pleaded. He centered himself in front of the girls, his eyes twinkling with eagerness as he rubbed his hands together.

"It will be an adventure ya won't want to miss out on!"

Chapter 3

Geoffrey Pierce, who turned out to be not only a friend of Miata, but also the inheritor of both a large estate and a large sum of money, seemed to be the most excited about the whole voyage. He spent all his spare time in preparation for their journey and, in fact, was so enthused about the event that he had an authentically fashioned Viking helmet made just for him to wear while aboard ship.

Not that he had any shortage of options of hats and helmets in his possession to choose from, but he elected not to risk something happening to them on their trip. In addition, he decided that the crew would refer to him as Viking Pierce. In his enthusiasm, he also bought the other four people in his party a couple new outfits of their choosing.

At the harbor, so fondly named Port of Sinking Ships by the French, the five instigators of this new voyage met to board their ship. The company comprised of a set of twins that knew nothing of their real origin, a thief with nothing better to do, a wealthy, slightly delusional dreamer, and his trusty butler who was wishing he could have opted to stay at home for the expedition.

As Mr. Bibbs set foot on the harbor, he clasped his hands behind his back and noted, "This has to be the most preposterous conglomeration of financiers the world of ships shall know in all the ages of eternity."

Bill, who was perched atop Jacq's shoulder, squawked out an agreement with the tall man, flapping his wings to emphasize the statement.

"Well said, good man!" Pierce exclaimed, blissfully ignorant of the meaning behind his butler's words.

Taking a long draw of the salty ocean air, Jacq felt her heart smile as the breeze picked up her hair, which hung free down her back beneath a rich blue bandana with six evenly placed coins dangling in front of her forehead. The sleeves of her new white blouse flapped in the small gust, greatly contrasting her dark bodice, black trousers, and boots. *If I did not love the sea,* she thought, listening to the soft tinkling of the coins she had transplanted from her old sash to her new one, *I would turn around right now.*

Not missing a beat, Pierce bellowed, "Welcome to the *Sea Dragon*! We be on our way to the great lands in the west! Now, follow me aboard our boat…er…ship…the *Sea Dragon*, to meet our captain and crew!"

Sighing heavily, Alex gathered the skirts of her new yellow dress and followed Jacq toward the ramp. Her parasol, open above her, matched the lacey gloves she wore on her hands. As they walked up the plank, she noticed her footsteps weren't near as steady as those of her twin. Setting her mouth and gripping her parasol, Alex took a firm first step on the deck—only to promptly lose her balance.

"Whoa there!" Miata's large hands grabbed her shoulder to steady her.

Alex recoiled immediately, stumbling again as she whirled to face him. "I'm quite fine!" she said as she brushed stray locks from her face. Miata in his new outfit filled her gaze. Never before having rightfully owned anything new in his life, the young man all but glowed with pride. In all actuality, all cleaned up, he looked like a different person.

He let a puff of air out his mouth. "I fear this to be a long voyage."

Bringing up the rear, Mr. Bibbs heard him and muttered to himself, "You have no idea..."

As they stepped on board, a gust of wind greeted them. Jacq inhaled deeply, her coins jingling louder as the breeze picked up, and smiled with pleasure at the beauty of the vessel. Everywhere she looked, she saw the crewmen working away, and she squealed with delight as she tiptoed around, forcing herself not to twirl about like a ballerina. She hurried to the portside rail and hung her head over to smile down at the deep waters. "Haha! I'm back!" Flapping his wings, Bill squawked down at the water and hopped off her shoulder, sweeping down closer to it.

"Ahoy, sailor! Back to work!" a voice hollered.

Jacq looked about for the shirker. When she did, she found a tall young man wearing a brilliant red blouse. Her mouth curving into a wry smile, she watched his dark eyes widen and his mouth open in confusion. Tilting her head to one side, she held out her hand for Bill, who returned to her. The man's lip curled, but he still had found no words to say to her.

Jacq threw her head back and laughed, too overjoyed to be back on a ship to take offense. "I'm not under your charge, sir. I'm one of the financiers of this voyage ... Well, sort of a financier ... more of an inciter, really ..."

Licking his lower lip, he nodded, taking in what she'd said. "Then I should ask of you a thousand pardons, miss," he replied, running his fingers through his loose black hair as calmly as if he had made only a very minor mistake.

"Nay, sailor," Jacq returned. "You can simply let me help when I ask if I may."

His brow knotted and he chuckled. "You, lass? I would hate for you to hurt yourself on a voyage you *incited*." Smiling at her in the same cocky way she had smiled at him, he turned on his heel and began barking out orders to the men on deck. Jacq's jaw dropped, and she narrowed her eyes at his broad back. But she said nothing and wandered back to her proper group of companions.

When she arrived, they were being introduced to the captain. "And this," Viking Pierce announced ever so loudly, "is Miss Alexandria Luray Thorpe, and her sister, Miss Jacqueline Luray Taylor. Jacq and Alex, this is our captain, Captain David Turner."

The captain, looking Jacq in the eye out from under his big hat, replied, "Thank you for the introduction, Mr. Pierce."

His dark eyes took her years back to a time when she didn't know she had a twin and when the seas were as accessible and flawless as her father and friend, Captain Taylor. Her heart fluttered strangely in her chest, almost making her choke.

"No harm shall come to them if my crew can help it."

Jacq smiled and bowed her head in a nonverbal thank you. Alex curtsied, and the captain was pleased. "Shall I do the roll call for you, Mr. Pierce?"

"Of course, Captain, if that is what ya should do next, then do so!"

The other four in his company forced apologetic smiles onto their faces. Taking a deep breath, Captain Turner patiently turned to his left, where a man of just over average height stood, looking smarter than at least half of the men aboard. He wore an embroidered tricorn hat and a fancy coat much like the captain's.

Seeing him, Alex inhaled sharply. Hearing this, Jacq's eyes grew anxious, and she mouthed, "I heard that." Alex smiled innocently, waving her sister off though turning pink in embarrassment.

"Jim!" the captain called. The man turned briefly for his introduction. "This is my first mate, James Monroe. Jim, read off the roll call, if you please."

"Aye aye, Captain!" Jim responded, turning to face the rail, though Jacq saw him steal a second glance at Alex before he did.

"I saw that," she mouthed, lifting her finger to point, though he could not see her. Alex elbowed Jacq and pushed her hand down. The sister sent her a narrow-eyed warning to be good.

"Roll call!" Jim's voice bellowed, louder than either of the twins thought possible. The men assembled onto the deck directly beneath the rail he was standing behind.

"Skippy Rackham."

"Aye!" Jacq saw the tall man in the red shirt answer. Tilting her head, she eyed him. He looked back at her and, catching each other, both turned away.

"Tom Thomas."

"Aye!" A man in a white shirt and black neck scarf waved at the twins.

"Benjamin Thames."

"Aye!" A strong man with a thick beard gave a nod.

"Scott Key."

"Aye aye!" A handsome man with a small ponytail and mustache gave a small wave.

Jacq sighed and looked far away, off at the distant horizon, where the sea met the sky, as far as her eyes could see. The breeze picked up again and moved her hair about, almost lulling her with its gentleness. Stepping silently away from the rest of the ship's officer crew in an almost trancelike state, she closed her eyes to the cool air and breathed deeply of it, letting her mind recall all the sweet memories of her past. As she let herself slip back into her childhood memories, she found herself asking why Captain Taylor—and why her original parents—had disappeared from her life. A tingly, warm feeling crept into her throat.

"Jacq," Alex whispered. Jacq cracked one eye to look at her sister. "Roll call's over. We're preparing to launch."

Jacq's eyes popped open, and, grabbing Alex and Miata by the hand, she raced to the prow of the ship, where a dragon successfully going into flight was carved as their figurehead. "Stand here," she directed them. "Feel the winds and the spray in your face as we depart from the seashore."

Alex and Miata looked at each other nervously and clung to the boat. Jacq traced the hand-carved wooden rail with her fingertips. Her coins jingled, and she fanned her fingers in the air. Skippy Rackham watched her from his place on deck. His friend, Tom Thomas, came along side of him. "That looks to be a fair one, eh?"

Skippy smiled innocently. "The wind?"

The young man rolled his eyes and snatched the end of a piece of rope nearby. "Nay, lad. Ye know what ol' Tom be speakin' of, and it ain't no wind." He grinned slyly and wound the rope throughout his fingers.

"I wouldn't know what else you were meaning, mate," Skippy insisted, shrugging.

"Lies!" Tom narrowed his eyes and shook his head. "Ol' Tom caught ye lookin' at the lass who loves the sea." Skippy looked over at his friend. "Aye, matey. Ye may be blind, but ol' Tom is not."

Shaking his head, Skippy turned his head back to look at the girl and sighed. "Tell me, Tom, how often do you see a lass that dresses as this one?"

Following, Skippy's glance, Tom shrugged. "Obviously ye have never been to the islands in the south!"

Skippy laughed a moment, then stared silently out to sea.

"Come on, now…" Tom fiddled with the rope in his hand. "What else be botherin' me mate?"

"You know what it is, Tom," Skippy said forlornly, staring out at the horizon as though it would give him an answer. "I don't think I should have taken this job."

Dropping the rope, Tom fumbled for words but found all he could do was open his mouth and close it again.

Staring at his boots for several seconds, he tried to concoct a proper response for his friend. "Skippy," he spoke after a pause of several seconds, "ol' Tom believes that ye shall do what be fittin' fer ye to do. Ye would be a fool to be doin' otherwise. So, if yer here, then yer meant to be."

The corner of Skippy's mouth lifted in thanks, but he said nothing as Tom turned and walked away. Picking up the end of rope Tom had dropped, Skippy breathed a belabored sigh. As he sat twisting the rope around his fingers, he suddenly felt hot, and he found that he had to clench his jaw to keep his eyes from tearing up. Once his friend was out of earshot, the lanky boatswain dropped the cord and walked to the rail of the ship and pulled a small pouch from within his shirt. Glancing about, he opened it, reached his hand inside, and produced red, velvety rose petals, which he very slowly let fall from his fingers onto the waves below.

Jacq, who had darted below to check out the room set aside for her and Alex, was staring idly out the small portal in their room when she suddenly saw the falling petals. Her heart jolted. Touching the glass with her fingertips as one of the velvety offerings drifted by, she whispered to Bill, "Oh, Bill ... Red rose petals ..."

Bill tilted his head and made soft clicking noises as though to ask her to explain. "Someone aboard this vessel is very sad. They must know someone who is very ill—or dying." She traced the edge of the window in a trancelike state as her eyes moistened. "That's what father ... well, Captain Taylor ... and I did for mother ... Before ... before she ..." Her voice stopped, and she tore her eyes from the drifting petals and fixed

them on Bill. He cooed remorsefully. Then, looking back to the window, she slowly eased herself to sit on the edge of her hammock. "May you both find peace with God."

As she lifted her feet to lie in the hammock, Bill hopped from her shoulder to sit on her feet. Cocking his head, he began to clean his toes. "Guh! Sometimes you are one of the most disgusting creatures that I know!"

Bill, a tail feather in his beak, looked up at her as if offended and blinked.

His antics lifted her out of the murky melancholy daze she'd temporarily become ensnared by. "Oh, I'm sorry, Bill." Holding out her hand, she added, "Isn't it exciting to be on a ship again?" Climbing willingly onto her out-stretched hand, Bill cooed and fluffed out his feathers.

"Ahoy, Jacq!" Miata called as he flung her door open. Bill flapped his wings and screeched.

Glaring at Miata, Jacq pulled the bird to herself in an attempt to calm him. "You'll need to get in the habit of knocking, you know... Alex won't take kindly to you bar-gin' in without permission."

"A thousand apologies." The man inhaled deeply, catching his breath. "We just got word that some o' us may be havin' to fill in as one o' them cabin boys."

"Why is this?" she inquired, sitting up so fast she nearly spun out of the hammock. Bill squawked and flew to a nearby ledge.

"It seems they can't find the boy anywhere on ship. They're thinkin' they be leavin' him at the docks somehow." Jacq's brow furrowed, and she leaned forward to hear more. "It appears to be the first time such a thing be happenin'."

Jacq frowned at the thought. "How did they manage that? How was this not realized afore we left the harbor? Isn't he a part of the roll call?"

"Aye." Miata sighed. "They be lookin' into what happened, but they also be wantin' us to work with the crew to make up for the absent lad."

"Three grown people to replace one lad?" Jacq asked, lying back in her hammock. "That does not add up correctly in my mind." Her brow furrowed.

"Well," Miata replied, scuffing his shoe on the boards, "it just be that Alex be havin' to fill in fer the other cabin boy who weren't anywhere to be found either, and they be wantin' me to be of assistance to the cook, Señor Torres." He smiled persuasively.

Leaning forward to get a better look at him, Jacq raised her eyebrow and inquired, "What are you saying, Miata? That I have no choice but to fill in for this other cabin boy?" She tilted her head in interest for his answer.

"*Squaw squaw squawk!*" Bill laughed, bobbing his head up and down and flapping his wings. Jacq lowered her lids at the bird.

"Well…" Miata sighed. "They were considerin' Mr. Pierce for the job, but bein' he be the one financin', and he be the one that be thinkin' he be a Viking descendent, they thought it be best to leave him to his own and allow Mr. Bibbs to watch him."

Jacq frowned but nodded in agreement. "Aye, that Geoffrey Pierce needs to be kept as far away from the sailing apparatuses as possible." Leaning back into the hammock, she held out her hand for Bill, who eagerly hopped on in want of attention.

"So, that be leavin' you, Jacq."

"Aye, so it do," she agreed, setting Bill on her stomach and starting to swing the hammock.

"I thought ye be the one that loved the sea? I thought fer sure if Alex be willin' to be lendin' a hand, ye would be more than happy to be helpin' out?"

"I do." Jacq raised herself up to nod vigorously. "I just have yet to love *having* to do something. It's much more enjoyable when you don't *have* to…" Miata nodded. "But, I will be along with Alex in hardly any time at all," she assured, lying back. Miata smiled thankfully, pausing a moment to watch her swing contentedly in her hammock, her pretty face glowing in satisfaction, before scurrying away to report the good news of her willingness to cooperate.

In less than a quarter of an hour, Jacq clambered back to the top deck. There, right in front of her, putting a net together, was Alex in her yellow dress. Her parasol was situated above her to prevent too much sun exposure. Grinning with amusement, Jacq pranced over and plopped down beside her sister. "How is it that you are doing this in that?" she asked, gesturing first to Alex, then to the net, and lastly to the dress.

Looking displeased over at Jacq, Alex inquired, "What are the odds that both of the cabin boys neglect to show up for a voyage *and* are forgotten at the harbor?"

Jacq grinned. "It's the food," she suggested.

Alex's expression faltered. However, Jacq's larger-than-life grin admitted to the joke, and she breathed a heavy sigh of relief.

"Ahoy, sailor!" a deep voice that Jacq knew she'd heard before called out. She turned to see Skippy Rackham, his arms crossed over his chest. Her mouth dropped open. She had to work under his charge? No, no! This would not do! "I'd like your help over here," he said, grinning.

Rising slowly to her feet, Jacq felt her eyes narrowing at him. She knew a grin like that. Bill flew to the crow's nest. Walking to him, she crossed her arms and replied, "What are you wanting my help with, sailor?"

His eyebrow moved up, and the corner of his mouth twitched. "First of all," he paused, looking her in the eye, "what am I to call you, exactly? Jacqueline?"

Jacq stifled a smile. "Well, if you really want, you may call me Miss Jacqueline Luray Taylor."

He blinked.

"Or, you can call me something shorter, like Jacq, if you wish. That is how I am known to most others I would call mate or acquaintance."

"I have no doubt you are known as such," he replied, looking her over skeptically, almost as though disapprovingly. The amused expression on her face dropped. "After all, Miss Jacqueline Luray Taylor is a rather long name." Grinning, he handed her a mop and gestured to the small deck below. "Just there, sailor," he ordered, then turned and sauntered off.

Grimacing at the mop, she mimicked, "Just there, sailor." However, she dropped down to the lower deck and began to swab as he had requested, a chore she had perfected over the years.

"Ye missed a spot," a voice pointed out rather brazenly.

"If you think you can do a better swab, then do it yourself." Shoving the mop to the dark-eyed sailor that had just approached her, she turned and marched off.

A little stunned with her reaction, he dropped the mop and followed her, saying, "Ho now, lass. Where be ye off to in such a t'underous state? Yer likely to sharpen a regular sword, ye are, with yer eyes gleamin' as such."

Stopping, she waited for him to catch up with her. "And who are you?"

"Name's Tom Thomas, but ye can just call me by me first name, and that be Tom. Ol' Tom can help ye out whenever ye need, Jacq," he confided in a low voice. "Just let me know if ye be needin' any help." Putting his hand on her shoulder, his tanned face split into a smile. "Or, if ye just want to have fun. I can see who ye be—a lass that loves the sea." He winked and walked away.

As soon as he was gone, she walked to the starboard railing and gazed out across the expanse of the sea and began humming her favorite tune, the tune she'd been humming the night Taylor had left her at the inn. Bill rejoined Jacq, and he listened intently as she continued more vocally with the tune until finishing, "*N is the north point that never points wrong, O are the orders of which we must be'ware, and P are the pumps that cause sailors to swear.*"

"Does your bird sing as well as you?"

Jacq twirled about, blurting, "What is it with men and eavesdropping?"

Skippy said nothing, only leaned against the rail. She decided to change tactics. Smiling sweetly, she asked, "Do you want me to swab another deck? If so, you should speak with Tom Thomas. He seems to have an eye for it…"

"Nay, Jacq." He sighed. "I just have not heard that song since my last captain died some years ago." Staring off out to sea, he mumbled to himself, "What a black night that was."

Jacq's heart leapt at this comment, for, of course, she had learned the song from her beloved Captain Taylor. Sidling up beside Skippy without getting close enough to touch, she watched him watch the sea. "A black night?" she repeated.

"The blackest." His stare and distant voice suggested he was still tortured by the memory of it.

"Was he a good man?" she whispered.

"The best."

"What was the name of your captain?" she found herself asking, though she had made a mental note not to do so.

Skippy's mouth twisted in a wry and woeful smile at the memories he had. "Captain Taylor. A big man with a bigger heart."

Jacq's eyes filled and her jaw trembled. Her heart beat in her throat so strongly she found it difficult to breathe.

"He never was satisfied in all the while that I knew him. It seemed there was a matter from before our meeting he'd left unattended, and it troubled him always."

Skippy glanced at Jacq and blinked several times at what he saw. The plucky lass, who seemed so confident and so bold, stood beside him near tears.

"I knew he didn't forget us." She turned her big, teary eyes toward Skippy. Her stomach churned so tumultuously, and her heart pounded so violently, she had to focus on not vomiting. "He wanted to take me to see the zebras of Africa." She choked.

Clouds began to roll in from nowhere. Skippy looked about in confusion. In all his time at sea he had never seen the weather change so drastically fast. "It's going to rain," she whimpered. Her breathing was shallow and labored.

Staring at her, Skippy sought for words, but found none. He watched as Bill blinked as if he had tears of his own, then nestled his beak into her soft, golden hair.

"You knew him?" he verified. She nodded. Smiling sympathetically, Skippy reached inside his shirt, pulling out his pouch of rose petals and, opening it, held it out to her. Staring into his dark eyes, she reached her trembling hand in, and when she felt the velvet pieces, she gasped and shook her head, retracting her hand. Reaching inside, Skippy pulled out a pinch of them. Taking her hand, he put half of them into her palm, and the other half, he held in his own out over the railing of the boat. Moving her gaze to his hand, she also held out hers, and as the newly formed clouds began to sprinkle large raindrops, Skippy and Jacq sprinkled rose petals onto the foamy waves of the sea.

"Who're these for?" Jacq asked as she let the last petals fall from between her fingers.

"A great lady." Skippy sighed softly. The rain began to fall heavier. "Why don't you come with me?" he offered, looking at the sky, then at the drenched girl. "I shall show you around." Smiling, she nodded and walked with him, amid the crew who was now rapidly trying to prep for the completely unexpected storm, toward the door to the lower decks.

Chapter 4

"So, who's Dante Rackham? Was that your father?" Jacq asked, standing on a crate to peer onto a shelf on which Skippy kept some of his belongings, looking at a compass with the name *Dante Rackham* elaborately inscribed into it. She twisted around to watch Skippy.

"What? Oh. Nay, lass. That's my real name. Skippy's the name most everyone in the ship business knows me by." He smiled at her as she handed the compass to him. The sprinkle several days ago had turned into a full-out downpour that lasted for a few days, and everyone had gone inside to get out of the rain. However, things were drying up and the sun was shining again. While they had been trapped inside for the majority of the time, a friendship, unexplainable for Jacq or Skippy, had formed between them, and they found they enjoyed each other's company immensely.

"Does anyone call you Dante? It's a nice name." Reaching into her pocket, she pulled out a cracker and gave it to Bill.

Dante shrugged. "You can if you want to. Mates and family call me by my real name most." Her smile broadened and Bill fluffed his feathers.

"Ahoy, mates!" Tom's voice rang out. Jacq turned her head, and Dante sat up in the hammock to see Tom bounding toward them, smiling.

"Would ye care to help me, lass?" he asked of Jacq. "We be needin' another hand fer the net on the upper deck."

"Of course," she said, stepping down from the crate.

As she walked past Tom, the sailor smiled over at Dante and winked. "We'll be seein' ya later, mate." Then he spun around and danced after Jacq as she climbed the stairs to the deck.

Dante could hear her giggle as Tom prattled, "One of the times me and me mates went fishing, we accidently pulled up fifteen starfish in our nets. Can ye fathom that? Fifteen starfish! Love, it was grand fun!"

"I can only imagine you with fifteen starfish!" Jacq laughed as she seated herself beside Alex, who was still managing to look prim and proper, though she was half-buried beneath the net. "Say, Alex, why do you think we were separated at birth? Do you think we were kidnapped?" Jacq huffed, out of breath from running up the stairs and forgetting Tom stopped behind them. It was maybe the millionth time the twins had had the conversation.

"And sold as slaves?" Jacq's eyes sparkled at Alex's suggestion. She laughed, rolling her eyes. "I think we have discussed that possibility before. Not likely, Jacq."

"Did you have any brothers or sisters? If you could call them brothers and sisters ..." Jacq picked up a corner of the net and began to check it over.

"No, I did not. And, are you checking over the net that I have already mended?" Alex stopped what she was doing and crossed her arms.

Turning her eyes guiltily to look at Alex, Jacq shook her head insistently. "I didn't know you'd already done this part!" Placing it down and picking up another section of net, she continued, undeterred, "So, I figure our last name is probably Luray. Do you think it was the name of our father? Or do you think it was the name of our mother?"

"Umm," Alex thoughtfully began looking over the net again, "I would guess that it was our father. Maybe our mother died."

"Could both of our parents have died?" Jacq asked, her face paling at such a possibility. It could not be so! Why had she suggested it? "Both of our guardians died."

"You do not know that mine died," Alex replied.

"Well, that's the only reason I can figure that she didn't come back for you," Jacq said, touching her sister's shoulder. "She was quite ill…"

Alex smiled softly. "Thank you, Jacq."

"Say," Tom chimed in, startling the girls, "be it possible that yer parents did not want to be losin' either of ye?" He smiled brightly, hoping to see some sign of positive hope shine from one of them. "Be it possible that there was a very unfortunate event that made partin' with ye mandatory?"

Glancing at each other, then back at Tom, the two girls shrugged. "You could be right, Tom. We have discussed this hundreds of times. We end up guessing at the same possibilities over and over again." Alex sighed, setting down the net. "The truth is, Jacq and I have no idea at

all what happened back then, and we may never see the people that knew again."

"Well, just fer the record, I be happy that things turned out as they did, aside from the fact that ye don't be knowin' who yer parents be, nor where ye came from, nor any other thing aboot yerselves than what ye know." An awkward silence filled the air around them. "Meanin' that I be glad that I be one of those who be knowin' ye." He smiled and looked at Jacq. "Yer such lovely lasses...An' if things were bein' otherwise, I may never be knowin' ye..."

Jacq smiled self-consciously and busily applied herself to patching a hole in the net. As she held it up to her face and looked through it at Alex, a low boom echoed in her ears.

"Ahoy, Captain!" the man from the crow's nest, Benjamin Thames, called down. "Cannon fire from a ship not far off!"

"Who be it shootin' at?" Tom asked, his face contorting in confusion.

"Not at us, that's for certain. They seem to be firing at a ship away to the north," Thames replied, peering through his eyeglass.

Jacq sprang to her feet, followed by both Tom and Alex, and ran to where Captain Turner stood, straining behind his telescope. "Who is what? I mean, what is that?" Jacq sputtered once she reached the captain's elbow.

His mouth turning in enjoyment of the girl's eager curiosity, he glanced down at Jacq. "The ship being fired upon bears the flag of a merchant ship. However, the ship doing the firing, I cannot see a flag atop its mast."

"Could it be pirates?" Jacq asked, grasping at the railing and dancing from one foot to the other.

"Of course not!" laughed Tom. "But," he continued as Jacq turned to face him with her brow furrowed, "if there be pirates, I will guard ye with me life."

"Pirates?" Alex inhaled sharply, causing Jacq to smile. Her voice was tinted with curiosity. Leaning toward Jacq, she asked in a low voice so as not to attract attention to herself, "How deadly are they in these waters?"

"Nary a man has seen a pirate in these waters for several months," Dante spoke evenly behind them.

"If there be pirates," Tom said, "I swear to ye, I shall do me best to protect both ye and yer sister."

Screeching to a halt just before he collided into the backs of the twins, Miata asked, "What be happenin' that I be needin' to know aboot?"

"Nothing." Jacq breathed slowly, hiding her excitement. "Except that there might be pirates about!" She grabbed his arms and focused all her energy on keeping herself from hopping up and down and her voice low.

"Pirates!" Miata repeated, sounding almost bewildered at the idea. "Followin' us? What be the cause fer that? Be they deadly?"

"Of course they are deadly!" Jacq's body trembled with anticipation.

"I do not know what you are so worried about," Alex said in irritation. Miata's eyes grew a little at this. Leaning close to him, she added, "After all, they are thieves..."

Miata smiled. "Aye, lass, but I be not a thief to travel aboot with other thieves, blowin' boats to bloody bits to get me gold..."

Nodding, Alex stuck out her lip and crossed her arms. "Good point."

Sashaying up behind them, Viking Pierce asked, "Am I hearing correctly there could be pirates?" The three turned to him, Jacq's eyes sparkling with adventure, Miata's clouded with concern, and Alex's laced with dread. "I take that to be an aye?"

"Mr. Thames!" Captain Turner called out, squinting up toward the crow's nest. "Do you have any idea what colors that other ship be sailing under?"

"Nay, Captain! They've yet to raise a flag, the lubbers!"

Heaving a deep sigh and glancing at the two girls, he finally hollered, "Mr. Briggs! Turn our course northeast. We're going to find out what's going on."

The wind did well behind the *Sea Dragon*, and it took them little time to arrive at their destination. Splintered wood and burning shards were strewn all across the waters. The assailed ship, *Steadfast Lula*, was a quarter of the way underwater. Smoke and steam filled the air, hovering closely above the water like a thick fog. The adversary, however, was unseen by even the keenest eye aboard ship.

"Ahoy!" Captain Turner hollered into the dismal sky. "Ahoy there! Is anyone here?"

"Excuse me! Halloo! Excuse me! Oh! I so don't want to shout ahoy. Excuse me! Halloo!" a nasal voice replied.

Squinting down into the smoke, Tom blinked. Leaning close to him, Jacq whispered uneasily, "Did you hear that?"

"Aye, lass," he said, looking down at her as she glanced up at him over her shoulder. "I be afraid so ..."

"Captain!" Thames crowed. "There be a rowboat off a small ways southeast o' us."

"Halloo!" the voice whimpered again. "Is there someone out there who is hearing my meek call for assistance? Halloo?"

Squinting into the dark, Jacq saw a well-dressed woman with frizzy, red hair floating in a rowboat. Tugging on Alex's skirt, she gestured toward her; Alex nodded.

"Ahoy!" Captain Turner called again. "You there, madam! Are you all right?"

"Yes!" she screeched back. "Those pirates! They attacked my ship! Stole my girl! Looted the crew! And left me here alone! I think they wanted me to die!"

"If they was wantin' ye dead, lass," Tom spoke up, "they would have killed ye theirselves!"

"Oh!" She clenched her little, gloved fists angrily. "Don't you call me lass, young man! You can call me Madam McLoflin, and that is all. Captain!"

Breathing a deep sigh, the captain winced and shouted, "Aye, Madam?"

"Would you please pull me aboard your ship! It's getting rather drafty down here! Those inconsiderate blackguards!" Pulling out a small lace hanky, she dabbed her eyes and started to sniffle.

Putting his arm around her shoulders, Tom whispered to Jacq, "Bringin' her aboard be the worst ting we done yet, me tinks." Seeing this gesture, Miata's lip curled in Tom's direction.

Her mouth turning in a rue smirk, Jacq whispered, "I think leaving her here may have the possibility of bringing about even worse results."

Soon, the woman was aboard the *Sea Dragon*, and as she was straightening her magenta-colored dress, Viking

Pierce stepped in to speak with her. "My, lass! Ye have bold red hair as I have never seen afore! How long will ye be with us on this voyage? Did ye know that we be on a treasure hunt?"

"A treasure hunt?" She gasped. "What kind of a ship *is* this? You are either fools in search of nonsense that does not exist, or you are pirates! Are you pirates too? Oh!" And with that, the strange woman with the vibrant red hair crossed her eyes, touched the back of her hand to her forehead, and slid into a frilly, crumpled heap.

Several hours later, the woman awoke to find Jacq and Alex leaning over her. "Oh! She is awake, Jacq!" Alex whispered. "There, there, madam." Alex smiled sweetly at her. "Sit up slowly and lean against this pillow. We shall get you a glass of water."

A weak smile shaped her lips. "Thank you, dear. I was having such a dreadful nightma … eek!"

Jumping at the woman's sudden outburst, Alex flipped about to see why the redhead was screeching. To her dismay, there stood Jacq, holding a tray with a cup of water and some oatmeal on it. The corner of Jacq's mouth curled in disgust at the woman, and she looked at her sister, raising her eyebrows in annoyance. Bill, perched on Jacq's shoulder, flapped his wings, irritated with the woman's obnoxious behavior.

"What is?" she cried. "Is that … a … a *pirate*?"

"Calm down, madam," Alex commanded shortly, taking hold of the woman's arm to keep her from flailing it.

"This is my sister, Jacq. She and I have been taking care of you since you fainted a few hours ago. And, no, there are no pirates aboard this ship."

Madam McLoflin eyed Alex for a moment and then stared at Jacq. "Why, if you are such proper young ladies, do you go by such strange names?" Wrinkling her nose, she looked over Jacq again.

Jacq, looking herself over, glowered at the redheaded woman. "Maybe because we want to. Has such an obscure thought never before entered your rubbish head?"

Alex's eyes grew and she shook her head at Jacq. Just then, Frank leapt onto the woman's feet at the end of the bed. "*Eek!*" the woman screamed. "What is that?"

"It's a monkey!" Jacq snapped, her voice coming out in a coarse rap. Handing the tray to the woman with over-emphasized elegance, she smiled at her, though her thoughts were quite opposite the gesture. Tromping down to the end of the bed, she then scooped up Frank and smiled down at the monkey, feeling a newfound fondness for him. "Have you never seen one of these before?"

Madam McLoflin was gripping Alex's hand tightly and gawking at Frank as though he was a rat that had just crawled out of the very sewers of London. "No, I have not," she hissed, staring at the monkey.

Hopping onto the top of Jacq's head, Bill twisted his head around upside down and looked at Madam McLoflin with one eye. Grunting in approval of Bill's actions, Frank wrapped his tail around Jacq's arm and hung upside down as well. Stretching out his fingers, Frank barely touched Madam McLoflin's leg. Throwing the tray up into the air, the woman let out an ear-ringing, "*Eeeeek!*"

Frightened by her actions, Frank leapt onto her lap and began to bounce around her. Bill flew into the air, squawking loudly. Alex jumped away from the side of the woman, landing beside her sister. The porridge and the glass of water went sailing through the air and crashed by the door.

Spinning to look at the two girls, a demand for help poised on her tongue, Madam McLoflin lost all speech as she found herself staring at identical twins, save their outer apparel, sucking in their lips to hide their smirks. She stared into their hazel eyes and saw two babies, wrapped in new linens to keep warm. She opened her mouth and then closed it again. Everything around her seemed to fade into a dreamy blur. All the noises of the animals were so distant. *Could it be?*

Finally, after a few seconds, she regained her senses and returned to yipping out her dissatisfaction. "Get these animals away from me!"

"Bill!" Jacq called. The parrot flew back to her shoulder and cooed. Alex held out her arm in front of the monkey, and Frank obediently crawled aboard. The two young women watched Madam McLoflin, her hair more frizzled than it had been before.

"Come, girls," she started, smoothing her hair, "tell me your real names. I'm sure they are much more delightful than these boys' names you go by."

"But much, much longer," Alex retorted, surprising Jacq. "I am Alexandria Luray Thorpe, and this is my sister, Jacqueline Luray Taylor." Jacq smiled and crossed her arms as she looked at the woman.

"You are sisters, but you don't have the same last name; you have the same middle name?" Madam McLoflin asked, sounding rather interested, but looking pale.

"Well, you see…" Jacq sighed, fidgeting at having to explain their predicament to this strange woman. "We don't know all the pieces. What we do know is that eight years ago, we were both brought to an inn at Port de Couler de Bateaux known as Midway Zebra. We are identical, and since we look undeniably alike and did both have Luray in our names, we have assumed that we are naught but sisters."

Bill nodded his head and squawked, "Sisters!"

"Oh!" Jacq giggled, reaching to rub the neck of the parrot. "He talked!" Clapping her hands, Alex offered the bird a cracker from Jacq's pocket. Madam McLoflin's paste-colored face paled even more. Her eyes emptied, void of all but one thought. Dark and stormy notions clouded her mind, leaving her face looking mortified. Seeing her expression, Jacq shook her head and muttered, "You don't get out much, do you?"

Staring at the twins, Madam McLoflin cried, "I think I'm still submerged in the very same nightmare that I have been in for what seems like a very long time! Amy! Amy, wake me up!" Flopping back onto the pillows, the woman began to whimper pitifully. Jacq and Alex looked at each other.

Viking Pierce, in his entire Viking outfit, waltzed in, followed by Miata. "Ahoy, lass! So sorry about earlier, I thought…"

"You again!" she squealed. "Who are you? Are you a pirate? Am I dreaming?"

While she was firing questions at Viking Pierce so fast he was unsure of what to say, her things, which were lying in a pile at the foot of her bed, caught Miata's well-trained eye. The young man scanned her possessions from afar, then, leaning down to admire something that particularly sparkled, he froze, realizing a strange silence had shut her up. Straightening, he saw her attention had flipped from Pierce to him.

"What are *you* doing? Are you...? Oh! Pirate! Thief! I *am* on another pirate ship, *aren't* I! Oh heavens! What have I done to deserve such ill will!" she squealed.

Jacq kicked Miata, and he glared at her. Alex glared at him, and he sneered at Madam McLoflin. Madam McLoflin stopped talking and stared at Viking Pierce. Viking Pierce, who, until now, had been stiff with shock, started laughing hysterically. "This," he declared, "is a wild one! It be so appropriate we found her driftin' in the sea!"

Grabbing the blankets on the bed, Madam McLoflin smothered her face in them and started to bawl.

"*Cak cak cak cak cak*," laughed Bill, wagging his head back and forth.

Viking Pierce, Miata, Alex, and Jacq stared at the sobbing woman for several seconds before Jacq leaned over to Alex and whispered, "Should we say something?"

Alex, her mouth twisted in thought, shook her head. "Nay, we should just let her cry herself to sleep, and wake up by herself."

"We could leave Frank here to watch her," Jacq offered, grimacing at the woman. Frank bared his teeth and growled.

Heaving a sigh at her sister's lighthearted suggestion, Alex replied, "I believe it is best we leave this woman alone. There is more here than we can help with."

"Aye!" Jacq muttered, chuckling to herself and covering her sides, knowing that Alex would wish to elbow her for her uncouth remark.

Shaking her head, Alex instead shoved her shoulder, almost tipping her over onto the floor. Suppressing her laughter, Jacq straightened and winked at Miata. At this, Alex shoved Jacq and the two boys out the door in front of her, leaving Madam McLoflin to her own devices.

"How'd it go?" Dante asked as Jacq leaned back against the starboard rail between him and Tom after leaving McLoflin's quarters. Jacq turned her eyes to him and blinked, twisting her mouth in a wry fashion while Frank hugged her waist. "That well, eh?" he asked, staring back in the direction of the wreckage they'd left to simmer in the water.

"Well, why they left her is as clear to me as why the French left Port de Couler de Bateaux," Jacq muttered.

Patting her on the shoulder, Dante gave her a small smile. "I'll go talk to the captain. He wanted to know how our new guest was faring."

"She's paranoid now," Jacq said, frowning. "She asked everyone except Alex if they were pirates. I think she hit her head on a board or something. What I can't understand though…"—she paused thoughtfully—"is why the pirates didn't just slit her throat and get it over with. Why leave her in a boat out in the middle of the ship's wreckage?"

"Not all pirates are cutthroats. Some of them have weaknesses." Smiling at her, he ran his fingers through his hair and added, "Just don't waste too much porridge on her. One of us might need it sometime."

Jacq's brow wrinkled, processing what he'd said as she watched him saunter off.

Tom sighed. "Strange lad. But aboot as nice as they be." Jacq gave him a short smile, then, setting Frank down, turned over and glared down into the ocean. Bill landed where Dante had been, shook his head, and began to preen. "Say, lass," Tom added, "don't be worryin' yer pretty little head aboot a mad woman such as that."

"Do you think I look like a pirate?" she asked, turning to look at him, her coins jingling with the swift toss of her head. The creamy white of her blouse, whose collar protruded contrastingly between the dark bodice and her throat, enhanced the growing tan of her skin.

He looked at the gold pieces hanging from her bandana and the sash around her waist and the adventurous sparkle in her eyes. "Nay, lass." He chuckled, looking closely at her smooth face. "Yer far pretty than any of the pirates I've ever afore met."

She smiled and her cheeks flushed a little. "Well, thank you, Tom." She shifted her eyes back out to sea, then glanced back at Tom, who was still looking at her. "Stop. You're embarrassing me," Jacq whispered.

"It be not embarrassin' to Alex when Jim be a lookin' at her," Tom retorted.

Jacq's mouth involuntarily tilted upwards; she choked on an amused laugh. "Alex does not know he is looking upon her," she responded.

Tom grinned. "So be it, Jacq. Let us be aboot our business for the ship now, eh?" he suggested. Then he also turned and wandered off.

Jacq exhaled heavily through her nose and stared far out to sea, farther, in fact, than possibly anyone had ever stared before. Shifting her weight, she let her brain churn carefully and mull over Madam McLoflin and her interest in her and her sister. It didn't make any sense. Neither she nor Alex recognized the woman; she knew that. If only they had someone they could turn to for these kinds of questions…parents…Someone they could trust no matter what…Her thoughts turned somberly to the Bumbleridges and their demise, Captain Taylor and his unfortunate end, and the mysterious disappearance of their birth parents—whoever they were…

Then, a smirk breaking her intense face, she giggled. Hopping atop her shoulder, Bill had picked up the end of her braid. As he examined it carefully in his birdlike way, he also was tickling her ear. Taking her hair from Bill, she chided, "This is not for you, sir."

"Sisters," Bill squawked, holding his foot out to her.

She laughed and let him crawl onto her hand. "Not quite, Bill. Not quite, but you can sure make me smile."

Turning to go inside, Jacq's smile suddenly fell. "Uh oh," Bill croaked. Jacq's face darkened. There, standing at the stern of the *Sea Dragon* and watching the wake, stood Alex and Jim, his arm around her waist. Frank reached up and grabbed Jacq's fingers. Scooping him up, Jacq giggled—though it was a sad sort of giggle—and whispered a bit sarcastically to Bill and Frank, "Looks like he's winning. What do you think?" Frank shook his head ferociously.

"No? Well, it looks like he is to me. Mr. James Monroe seems to be a very nice man. He's never mean to Alex," she explained to Frank, "and I don't think he'd ever leave her."

Bill snorted through his nose. Smiling, Jacq turned, almost running into Miata.

"Jacq," he whispered, glancing at the waning sunlight. "There be somethin' I be wantin' to talk to ye aboot."

Handing him the monkey, she nodded, saying, "Go on."

"It be that, after much contemplatin' aboot what ye said afore we left, I be believin' that me mate didn't translate yer lockets properlike." He scuffed his boot on the deck.

Jacq felt the corner of her mouth raise in curiosity. "Go on."

Chapter 5

"So, you see, there could be a problem." Jacq swung in her hammock watching Bill hold his wings out to keep his balance.

"Aye. There could be a big problem." Staring thoughtfully at the ceiling, Alex ran her fingers through Frank's beige fur. After several seconds of silence, she murmured, "What are we to do about it?"

"I'll try to translate it. If they were pirates, I agree with Miata that they wouldn't have left such an obvious trail to their treasure. Miata said that he was skeptical of Pierce's translation from the beginning, just because he's been so badly wanting adventure. I just don't know where to begin. Do you think it should rhyme, being it is a riddle?" Rolling her head around to look at Alex, Jacq peered at her from the corner of her eye, hopeful she would agree with her guess.

"Aye, Jacq. I think that is a good start." Another moment of silence ensued. "How sure are you Miata is right about this?"

"He wouldn't have told me if he didn't really think so. I trust him…" Jacq cast an honest glance at Alex to reassure her.

"Aye. A fact that baffles me," Alex noted, ending her statement with a small huff.

Jacq smiled, knowing her exasperated statement was not at all exaggerated and actually quite serious. "We shall not tell anyone aboard the ship, that way, if we are wrong, then no harm is done. If Pierce is wrong, then we have another possibility to look for."

"Agreed."

"That means we can't tell anyone. Not even Captain Turner."

Alex nodded.

Eyeing her closely, Jacq added, "Or Jim Monroe…"

Smiling at Jacq with slightly narrowed eyes, Alex's lips parted and then closed, the smile taking on a hint of a glare to it. "Of course."

"Girls!" Madam McLoflin's voice rang out. "Girls! Please don't leave me with the dreadful men aboard this ship! It's not right, I tell you!" The redheaded woman burst into their room, sending the bird and the monkey into the air.

Jacq snorted. "The men aboard this ship are not that dreadful, madam. I'm sure they feel the same about you that you do about them."

"Why! Of all the nerve! If your parents were here, I would be sure they would hear of this outrageous speech! My word! The nerve!" Her voice climbed in pitch, and Jacq scowled at the floor.

Alex stared broken-heartedly at the woman standing cold and haughty before them. "I think," she muttered, stumbling over her words, "that is quite possibly the harshest thing you could have said to us." Her eyes darkening, Alex could feel an emotion she was not well acquainted with rising up in the core of her being. The audacity this woman had to speak to them so! She waved her hand dismissively. "You may go now."

Wordlessly, she held her hand out to Frank, who crawled onto her arm and then into her lap. Alex admired his little black face that had never said anything so painful to hear. As she reached down and touched his fur, he cuddled up to her, and with the same smooth, soft motion, touched her face with his hand, his large eyes pleading for her to feel better.

"I'm sorry," the woman mumbled. "Did you ever know your parents?"

"Nay," Jacq's muffled voice answered.

"Oh." The woman fidgeted. "That is quite unfortunate. You seem to have grown up rather well without parents."

Jacq listened keenly now. "Thank you." Her eyebrow rising in interest, Jacq added, "So, who is Amy?"

Madam McLoflin said nothing.

"You called for her when you decided that you were dreaming."

Still nothing.

"Is she your daughter?" Jacq pressed.

Madam McLoflin was staring, wide-eyed and speechless, at the girls. "Amy," she responded slowly, "is like a daughter to me. I'm her governess."

Jacq rolled over and leaned forward in one smooth motion, looking hard at the woman. "You're a…a… governess?"

Her trancelike state snapping at that comment, Madam McLoflin straightened. "Do you think I would not be a good governess?"

Catching Jacq's eye, Alex shook her head. Jacq looked at Madam McLoflin, who stood awaiting the answer. "Well," Jacq returned thoughtfully, "you just seem a little jumpy." There was an awkward silence. "For a governess."

Her brow furrowed, and she glanced at Alex for assistance. Alex smiled sweetly and, laughing uneasily, continued for Jacq. "Aye, you seem like a well-bred woman who would have a governess for her own children."

Madam McLoflin swelled with pride and shone like the sun. She seemed tall and grand with her fiery red hair and pale throat. Jacq and Alex exchanged glances. "Well, thank you, girls.…." She looked them over again. "I am going to retire for the evening. If anyone needs me, you know where to find me." She curtsied with poise and then strode out of the room, her head up, her strides long.

As she closed the door, Jacq looked over at Alex, her brow furrowed, simpering, "A governess?" Falling back into her hammock, she roared with laughter. "Please! If anyone like her arrived in Port de Couler de Bateaux, *that* is why the French left! Hahaha!"

Alex grinned over at Jacq swinging her hammock. "One of these days, you are going to swing that thing too far, and it is going to fall off."

"Nay, lass. It shan't." She began to kick harder in jest.

"Aye, lass. It shall!"

"Shan't."

"Shall."

"Shan't."

"Shall."

"Shan't."

Thump!

"Hahaha!" Alex laughed as Jacq winced and got up to fix her bed.

"Captain!" Thames's voice broke the still quiet early the next morning.

"Aye, Mr. Thames?" Captain Turner's deep voice answered.

"There be a ship behind us on our port side!" he called down, leaning out of the crow's nest.

"How far off is she, Mr. Thames?" He stood beside the helmsman, Mr. Briggs, clasping his hands behind his back.

"She looks to be aboot a quarter of a day behind or so." Putting the telescope down, he peered off into the distance. "She be hardly visible without a telescope, and with one, she be barely recognizable as a ship."

The captain sighed, making his way to the stern. "Very well, Mr. Thames. Keep an eye on her, two if you can spare the other."

"Aye aye, sir," Thames answered, gazing out into the rest of the open waters.

"Captain," Jim Monroe's calm voice interrupted as he came to a stop at the captain's side.

Holding his position, not turning to face his first mate, Captain Turner let out a short, pensive exhale then acknowledged him. "Aye, Jim?"

"Do you fear it to be a pirate ship … just between me and you?" He stood like the captain, his hands clasped behind his back, staring out to sea.

"I don't know. That's what worries me," Captain Turner answered, glancing toward the first mate. "But we shall know soon enough; you can bet your boots to that."

"Do you think that it's ill luck from having women aboard?" asked Dante, coming up behind the two men.

"Nay, Mr. Rackham. There is no such thing as ill luck." Turning in unison, the boatswain and first mate gaped at their captain. Noticing their glances, his face creased and he chuckled. "Well, there's not, lads. The closest thing to ill luck is a bad storm when there are no clouds in the sky."

Exchanging glances, the two young men smiled at this explanation. Satisfied, they rejoined their captain gazing out at the sea.

"Do we tell the rest of the crew if we discover her to be pirate?" Dante inquired, adjusting his vest.

"Nay." Captain Turner sighed, tugging on his hat. "If we find her to be pirate, then we shall act as swiftly as we can and wait until the last possible moment to concern our crew and guests. A conflict should be avoided at all costs."

"Aye, Captain," Dante agreed, with every intention to follow his captain's orders.

"Dismissed, lads," Captain Turner announced. Turning, the captain headed off on his usual morning patrol walk along the portside rail of the ship.

"Jim." Dante gave the first mate a nod, clasping his hands behind his back and bending respectively at the waist.

"Skippy," Jim returned, performing the very same physical gesture. Pivoting on his heel, Monroe moved off to perform his morning patrol of the starboard rail.

Stretching as soon as the first mate had gone on his way, Dante hopped over the inner railing of the platform deck, landing on the deck below.

"Careful," he heard behind him as he hit the deck.

Without turning, he asked, "Why? Are you afraid you might spill?" He turned to see Jacq sitting against the wall, holding a cup of something warm and turning her head to look again at the early sun. "You're astir a might early this morning, aren't you?"

"Aye. I couldn't sleep," she answered, moving her gaze down to her drink.

He crossed his arms and stared out at the horizon. "Were you thinking about Tom?"

"Nay!" she retorted, meeting the sound of disgust in his voice with hers.

"Oh. Well, I know I wouldn't be able to sleep thinking of him, so I was just wondering," Dante said, grinning down at her with his sarcastic humor glinting at her from every line in his face.

"Is that so? Who helps you go to sleep? That great lady of yours?" Jacq sneered.

Dante's smile faded, but he quickly picked himself up again, saying, "No, I find that if I think about myself, I go to sleep the fastest."

"Are you related to Narcissus?" she asked playfully.

"Of course not!" Dante laughed, sliding down the wall to sit beside her. "It's because I'm boring." With that, he sprang back to his feet and started to saunter off.

"Dante!" she called after him. He turned. "I shall speak with you later."

He bowed, flinging his arm about with sardonic eloquence. "As you wish." Then off he was, in a hurry.

Clambering up the stairs, Tom burst forth from the hatch in the floor a small distance in front of Jacq, followed by Pierce, singing, "*Ahoy diddle diddle! A cat played a fiddle, She knew a cow who could jump to the moon, She knew a dog who laughed at any riddle, And he knew a fish that swam to Spain with a spoon!*" Tom flopped down next to Jacq and gave a grin that screamed he was indubitably happy.

Pierce fell down on the other side of her. "Someday, in one of the sports I create that shall be famous, they will name a team after me! The Vikings they shall call themselves! And they shall be victorious!" he declared, sitting up against the wall.

Jacq stared at him, her mouth opening as though she wanted to say something. However, she found that she could think of nothing suitable to say. Squinting over at where the sun sat in the fresh sky, she turned to Tom and asked, "What are you lads drinking at this hour?"

"Nothin' that ain't good fer the soul!" Tom whispered loudly to her. "Ol' Tom can fix ye up if ye wants as well! I be willin' to share with ye today!"

Jacq shook her head. "You fools were down in the kitchen again, weren't you?"

"Pedro said we could have some!" Viking blurted, smiling in the sunshine. In a few seconds, he was fast asleep.

Jacq glared over at Tom. "You aren't, are you?" she questioned him doubtfully, taking a sip of her own drink.

"Nay, lass!" He laughed. "I just be wantin' this lad to settle hisself down, 'ats all." He smiled over at Viking and then leaned back, adjusting the black knotted cloth around his neck. "How be ye this morn?" he asked. "Yer lookin' as lovely as the flowers of spring."

"I'm feeling just fine, thank you." Eyeing him, she took another sip. "Tom? What is your position aboard this ship?"

"Aboard this here ship? What be ol' Tom's job, eh?" Chuckling, he pulled a chunk of bread from his belt and replied, "To eat o' course! And be entertain' ye, lass." He took a big bite of the bread, and when he swallowed, he asked, "Why be ye askin'?"

Watching Dante talk to a couple of the crewmen, Jacq shrugged and replied, "Just wondering."

Turning to gaze at her, Tom started to speak, but was interrupted by a voice.

"Ahoy there, Miss Taylor!" Captain Turner bellowed from the prow. "I'd like a word with you."

Patting Tom on the shoulder, she hopped up and trotted over to the captain. "What is it, Captain?"

"You've been at sea afore, have you not?" he spoke smoothly when she stood motionless beside him.

"Aye, Captain."

He smiled at her short response. "Who did you sail under, Miss Taylor?"

"I sailed with Captain Taylor," she replied, the smile that had been gracing her face dipping down slightly at the corners.

"Was he your father?" Captain Turner eyed the girl closely as he asked his question.

"Not by blood." She sighed, looking down at her shoes. "But he treated me as though he was, and I thought of him as such."

"As I would expect from Daniel," the captain stated, nodding as he watched the water swirl in their wake. "He lived a good man, and he died a good man. I haven't met a better one in all my travels."

"I knew he was a good man," Jacq replied, scuffing her boot. "And I was heartbroken to learn that I had misread his reasons for not coming back to get me."

"Don't be kicking yourself because you made a mistake. Sometimes angels fall. Not a soul, save our good LORD, is perfect. Always remember that. The trick to life is to get back up again." With that, Captain Turner about-faced and marched away to tend to other matters.

Smiling at his back, Jacq sighed and then hurried down below. Shutting the door securely behind her, she snatched up her bag, dumping the contents onto the floor. As she did so, the pistol spilled out along with the blank parchments she had stuffed into her bag. Inhaling sharply at the sight of it, Jacq knelt and scooped it up in her hands, running her fingertips across its smooth surface. Gripping the handle, she held it up at eye level as though aiming at a spot on the wall. *That's it, Jacq . . .* she heard Captain Taylor's voice in her mind. *Great shot! I think you just might be a natural.* She remembered smiling gleefully at his praise before handing his gun back to him.

Then, blinking away the memory, she shoved the firearm back into the bag and pulled out the lockets, forcing

herself to focus on the task at hand. Opening up the two charms, she reread the lines to herself and shook her head. "*At the SW sea, turn your back, to the inn*," she muttered, "*lies the key, Across the way*." On a piece of paper she'd placed on the floor beside herself, she jotted down 'sea' and 'key.' She scratched the side of her head with the end of the pen. "Why is the capitalization on these odd?" she murmured, staring at the second line. "Maybe it's divided in half ... Move *Across the way* to the front and *lies the key* to the back ..." Sitting back against the wall, she twisted her mouth in thought.

Bill jumped down onto the floor beside her and stared down at the words. "Sisters," he squawked, fluffing his feathers and marching across her things.

Jacq looked at him curiously, then murmured, "If it rhymes ..." She scribbled a little. "And has to make sense, of course ..." She twisted the pen and scribbled more. "*At the inn, turn your back, to the SW sea*. It just might work." She laughed, writing it down. Bill nodded his head, knocking his beak on the wood.

"Jacq," Alex whispered, opening the door and poking her head inside, "come quickly."

"What is it?" Jacq asked, dropping the pen and scooping up Bill.

"It is Madam McLoflin. She is asking to see us." Alex peered at the paper and the open lockets Jacq had on the floor.

"Is she dying?" Jacq inquired, putting on her locket and holding the other up to Alex as she shoved all the rest of her things into a pile.

"I do not know, just come on!" Grabbing her locket from Jacq, Alex put it on and waited for her sister.

They hurried to the room of Madam McLoflin and were surprised to see her standing, facing out the window. The two exchanged glances and then returned their gazes to Madam McLoflin. "Halloo, girls," the redhead greeted them coolly. "I am delighted that you have arrived so soon after I requested to see you." She did not turn to face them. She remained staring out the window, her back as straight as a well-carved pole. "There is something that I need to tell you. Hopefully, it will set your hearts to rest, at least a little."

Squinting, Jacq could see the woman's pale reflection in the window. She was wringing her hands together like mad. Tilting her head at this, Jacq turned a keen ear to what Madam McLoflin had to say.

"If you are who I have come to believe you to be, then you are the twins of Mr. Luray and his wife, under whom I worked for a number of years of my young life. After you were born, both of your parents contracted consumption and they died, leaving you in my charge. However, I was very young at the time, much too young to care for children, and I could not take care of you myself. I gave you to a nice couple—family friends, as it were. Alas, they were not as good as they seemed. They separated you and sold you off. I was devastated to hear this horrible news, but there was nothing I could do to right the wrong. I am indeed glad to know you are both alive and well." Still, she did not face them.

"What were our parents' names?" Jacq asked, watching the woman with an unwavering gaze. Alex gripped her arm.

"Your mother's name was Mary," Madam McLoflin's voice spoke again. "It was so long ago, and I was so young. I do not remember your father's name."

Jacq raised an eyebrow. "How old are you now, Madam McLoflin? You look as though you've yet to reach the age of thirty." Jacq's eyes glinted at her question, and Alex took notice of her devious expression.

Glancing back at Jacq in gratitude for the comment, Madam McLoflin started to smile, then returned to staring out the window. "Thank you, dear, but I will turn thirty-nine within the year." Her voice had a downcast tone to it, though it was well oiled with smooth, eloquent style of speech.

Nodding thoughtfully, Jacq then made a terse bow. "Good afternoon, Madam McLoflin." Shutting the door securely behind her, she marched off in the direction of the prow. Her lips were tight, and her face looked dark.

Her forehead wrinkling in distaste as Jacq shut the door to Madam McLoflin's room, Alex curtsied in her graceful manner. "Thank you, Madam McLoflin, and good day." Turning on her heel, Alex walked to the door and, though closing it gently behind her, ran to catch up to her sister. "Jacq! Jacq, what was—"

"She's bluffing, Alex!" Jacq's voice was firm and her accusation resolute as she spun around, gesturing toward the closed door. "She didn't look at us the *entire* duration of the story."

"Maybe it gives her much pain to this day," Alex said.

Almost reeling back at this, Jacq sputtered, "Too much pain? If she was so upset about it, why can't she remember the name of our father? Not just that, but she's thirty-eight, and we're eighteen. Do the math!" Casting a menacing glower once more in the direction of the redheaded woman's door, Jacq tossed her hair and stormed off.

Alex started, blinking in shock at her sister's heated opinion on the matter. "Thirty-eight," she mumbled, looking at the deck. "Eighteen." Her mouth twisted as she watched Jacq's retreating figure.

Cramming herself down into the forward-most part of the deck, Jacq stared out to sea. "Not old enough ... what a bloody lie ..." she muttered.

"Ill luck, lass?" Tom's voice interrupted her thoughts. "Or just ill news?"

"I don't know yet," she replied, undoing the end of her braid.

"Just let ol' Tom know if ye be needin' anythin'," the sailor reminded, touching her shoulder eagerly. "I'll be below for a few moments, relievin' Señor Torres of some of his fruit." Winking, he turned and strode off.

Listening to his boots clunk away, Jacq laid her forehead on her hands piled on top of each other on the railing.

"There's no such thing as ill luck ..." Dante's soothing voice breathed near her, interrupting her thoughts after a few moments of hearing nothing but the quiet din of the crew and the eager splash of the ocean.

"Nay?" Jacq questioned, not moving.

"Nay. The closest thing to ill luck is a bad storm when there are no clouds in the sky," he recited, gazing up at the nearly cloudless sky.

"That sounds beautiful." She picked up her hair again, unbraiding it methodically as she listened to his voice.

"When I found out that my mother was ill, I didn't want to believe them. She had always been a pale, thin woman, but she always had such a grand smile, and she could laugh..." He paused. "She could laugh..." Chuckling for a moment, he sniffed and lightly touched his side where he'd stored the rose petals. "It took me a long time to accept that she was ill, and I just recently have come to believe that it wasn't ill luck that was behind it."

Glancing at the drawn expression on his face, Jacq's heart fell. Her lower lip trembled and quite suddenly, she felt the size of a mouse. Reaching out her hand toward him, but not touching him, she felt her mouth twitch open and heard her voice say, "I'm sorry. I did not know of your mother's illness."

Shaking his head, Dante replied, "You needn't be sorry. I didn't even tell you, for it matters not. What is troubling you?"

"Heh," Jacq blurted in half-hearted laughter. "I cannot say." Having finished releasing her hair from its bonds, she flung the free locks over her shoulder. Stretching straight out behind her, they danced in the breeze as the coins jingled joyfully along with them.

Dante stepped nearer to her. "Why not?"

She could feel his body heat, he was so close, and she wondered if it was really Dante, or if it was Tom. Turning, she came nigh on face to face with the handsome boatswain. Her soft eyes took in his thin, angular face. He'd started to open his mouth when she turned, but closed it and only smiled at her. "Ummm...because...I do not

even know for certain. And I would hate to be thought a suspicious fool." She gripped the rail behind her as her breathing became slightly more shallow.

"Fear not," Dante whispered in his deep, husky voice. "The thoughts of others often mean little in comparison to our own." Staring deep into his eyes, she nodded in acknowledgement of what he was saying. "Take care, Jacq," he concluded, then turned to march away.

"Thank you, Dante," she whispered in too low a tone for him to hear. Swallowing a hard lump in her throat, she watched him cross over to talk to one of the men. It wasn't until he was several steps away that she realized she could hardly breathe and her heart was fluttering in her chest.

"Swarthy an' 'andsome, ain't he, lass?" Tom's voice broke in. "'Tis what the ladies be lovin' aboot me mate, Skippy." Tom sighed, looking back and forth a couple times between Dante and Jacq. He took a bite out of the apple he had retrieved.

"Oh, Tom," she pleaded in a voice so desperate it almost cracked when she spoke his name. "Tell me what to do. I know not what to believe." She sighed, looking across the ship. Alex stood near Jim, talking with him intently. Jacq could see Alex fidgeting and gesturing toward the sea in the direction they'd come. Jim kept trying to touch her shoulder or her elbow, but neither held still long enough for him to put a reassuring hand on them.

Reaching to Jacq's face, Tom touched her cheek and held her chin. "Why be the lovely Jacq so beset with worries?" he inquired, tilting his head. Closing her eyes at his voice, Jacq leaned into him, and he embraced her, his face forming a smile of delight that, had Jacq seen it, she might

have slapped him for. "There, there, lass," he soothed, swallowing his mouthful of fruit. "There be nothin' to worry aboot in ol' Tom's arms. Of that, ye can be sure."

Glancing back at them over his shoulder, Dante saw Tom, who winked, and very softly under his breath, he chuckled as the taller man looked away.

Chapter
6

"Skippy!"

Dante stretched in his hammock. "Aye, Tom?" He yawned, fluffing his hair by running his hand back and forth across the top.

Tom reached his hammock, stopping abruptly and staring at his hair sticking up every which way around his head. Dante stared at him blankly. "Ol' Tom be likin' the looks o' yer hair like that," he commented.

Grinning, Dante replied, "What is it you want, Tom?" Lying back, Dante swung the hammock back and forth, watching Tom as he did so.

"I be wantin' ye to come help me with somethin', Skippy."

Rubbing his eyes with his fists, Dante yawned again, stretching lazily. "And why are you not asking Jacq to help you? You've been asking her to help you with everything else as of late."

"This be somethin' no lady be doin' willin'ly in front o' a bunch o' men." Tom jittered from one side to the other of Dante's bed, the light in his eyes dancing like a

candle flame. Sitting up, the boatswain smiled. Nodding with a smile as wide as his face, Tom added, "There be no breeze today."

Several minutes later, the two, along with a few of the other crew members, were out in the sea. A rowboat occupied by Charles Pitt, usually a rather stodgy fellow, bobbed about in the waves as the rest of the men swam around him in the waters. Jacq and Alex watched them over the railing for a short while, waving and snickering at Miata, Tom, Dante, Jim, and the rest of the young sailors until Jacq suddenly remembered her side project she had unintentionally left idle for the last couple of weeks. At this, she discreetly excused herself from Alex's side, turned, and hurried down below to the room the two girls shared. Pushing aside her things, she made a small space on the floor and pulled off her locket to look at it again. Coming down from the rafters above her—his new favorite place to nap on the ship, Bill sat on the edge of the hammock until he found the balance of the thing not to his liking, then he hopped onto the top of her head. "Bill," she muttered, "must you sit on the top of my head?"

Her attention, however, was drawn to the locket and the paper, and she hardly noticed him say, "Aye-aye."

She sat for several minutes. "Sea. Key." She stared at the engraving for a long while, tapping her jaw with the pen. "Across the way lies the key." Turning to her notes, she reread both lines together: *At the inn, turn your back, to the SW sea / Across the way lies the key.* Her jaw moved in thought. "Turn your back to the southwest sea," she repeated. Shoving all of her things away, and almost knocking Bill off, she jumped up, put the locket around

her neck again, grabbed up the compass she'd been given, and ran to the upper deck. She flew to the rail, and Bill flew off her head.

Staring down at the foamy waves splashing up on the sides of the vessel, she felt a shiver run down her spine. Flipping open the compass, she stared down as the needle spun to point north, verifying they were indeed headed southwest. "We were never supposed to leave the harbor," she whispered.

"Jacq," Alex's voice broke in. Jacq turned shakily, clapping the compass shut and shoving it into her pocket. "What is the matter with you?"

Shaking her head, Jacq looked back out to sea. "Our journey should not be across the waters," she murmured.

"You know this?" Alex inquired, sidling up beside her twin and harmonizing her pitch with Jacq's. Jacq nodded. Landing on her hand as it grasped the rail, Bill shook his head. Alex's eyes widened. "How?"

Putting Bill on her shoulder and opening her locket, she whispered, "At the inn, turn your back, to the southwest sea / Across the way lies the key."

Alex stared at her sister and then at the locket. Reaching out her hand, she grazed the locket's golden inside with her fingertips. "Whatever shall we do?"

"We shall say nothing of this to anyone," implored Jacq, grabbing Alex by the shoulders. "We may be wrong, though this I doubt. Black Fred and Golden Jem were no fools. They were smart folk who could read and write just as everyone else. They would not have made this a map otherwise. Besides," she sighed, looking off to the starboard side of the ship, "there are pirates out there."

Alex turned large eyes toward her sister. "What makes you so certain?"

"Why else would they leave a woman amongst the debris of a ship? Why would they want us to turn back, other than an easy way to catch up?" Releasing her sister, Jacq moved back to the portside rail, overlooking where the men were finishing swimming and climbing back into the rowboat. Her eyes narrowing, she gazed out at the horizon. "They're out there, just waitin' for us, lass."

Nodding, Alex sighed. "Very well. I accept your theory, but what do we do?"

Jacq's mouth curled upward impishly, all her childish devilry resurfacing in one expression. "We wait."

Below them, Tom and Miata listened to the sounds of the boat. "Beautiful, isn't it?" Miata murmured, holding a gold coin like the kind Jacq had strewn on her bandana and sash in the air above him.

"Aye, that she is, lad. It be bogglin' me mind how ye be managin' to be stayin' her mate all these years without harborin' desire," Tom spoke as he started pushing his mop again. The morning's recreation over, it was back to work for all able-bodied men aboard.

Miata's forehead wrinkled at his response. Shoving the coin back into his pocket and rolling his eyes, he muttered, "Useless. Yer utterly useless. Wastin' yer dreams away on a lass ye shall ne'er be havin'. She be deservin' more than the likes o' us. An' if she not be havin' me, she certainly not be havin' ye!" Bending down, he snatched up his mop

and dunked it into the nearby bucket, casting a disgusted glance toward Tom Thomas.

Turning, Tom watched Miata slosh around the water on the floor for a few moments. "Oh ... ye be gettin' turned down, eh, mate? Most unfortunate fer ye ... But, be ye not believin' ol' Tom be worthy o' yer mate?" he challenged.

Twisting back, Miata took a step toward him. "I be believin' there be but a might small number o' men worthy o' me mate, Tom." The young man's voice came out both even and smooth. "Ye not bein' one o' 'em be what I said, mate, and I be meanin' it."

Down the stairs from where they stood, Viking Pierce bellowed, "Mr. Bibbs! Get me another glass o' ale, ol' boy! Mr. Bibbs! Where in t'underation have you gotten to? Mr. Bibbs!" Tom and Miata turned to stare in the direction from which Viking Pierce's voice was erupting.

A figure rose from the staircase behind them. "I agree with Miata," a voice noted. Turning to see who it was, the two jumped apart as Mr. Bibbs brushed between them, saying, "Pardon me."

"Be ye thinkin' he be knowin' who we was talkin' aboot?" Tom inquired, leaning on his mop and glancing over at Miata, who was still staring curiously down the stairs after Mr. Bibbs.

"I know not," Miata said, "but the other lass be a proper lady and be deservin' o' a good, honest man as well." Throwing one last glance back at Tom, his lip curled at the corner and he fidgeted a moment with his mop. "No blood?"

Bowing, Tom responded coolly, "No blood."

At this, Miata trudged up the stairs, letting his mop bump along behind him. As he reached the top of the stairs, he all but ran into Alex. Inhaling sharply, Alex barely stopped herself from knocking James Monroe over to try and avoid Miata. After the two recovered, he smiled knowingly. "A thousand pardons," he offered in a soft voice, and then off he danced, his mop thrown over his shoulder.

Alex and James watched him for several seconds before they turned to each other. "As you were saying," James prodded, smiling down on her.

Feeling her cheeks getting a little warm, Alex stared down at his feet. Twirling the parasol she had positioned over her shoulder, she shyly pulled her lower lip under her top teeth. "I was just saying how lovely I think it would be if I could learn a little more. I disbelieve I shall ever attend any kind of school again, but learning on my own would be so very lovely. It would be delightful, would it not?"

Watching her mouth move and her eyes dance, Jim's smirk broadened. "I think you could do anything you wanted to," he returned. "Personally, I'd like to settle down in the near future." Pausing, he observed her as she looked at him with an expression he could not read all too well. His smile decreased.

"Settle down?" As she asked for verification of his term, she spoke softly, as though she was afraid if she spoke too quickly or too loudly, he would run away. Her eyes, big and warm, scanned his face desperately.

"Aye." Feeling surer of himself, he returned his gaze straight into her eyes. "You know, marry a wonderful lady and start a family."

Her mouth twitched, and Alex whispered, "Would not that be just lovely?"

His smile growing in breadth and boldness, he tucked a tiny stray golden lock away behind her ear to join it with the rest of her hair. "It would."

As they stood, each basking in the glow of the other, forcing themselves to keep proper distance, Jacq noticed them from where she sat on the figurehead of the bow. Smiling soberly and distantly sad, she noted to Bill, who sat on her knee, "Pity. I thought we were going to travel the world together... See the zebras..."

Cooing, Bill bobbed his head. Reaching her hand out, Jacq touched his feathers with her fingertips and watched him close his eyes. Sighing, Jacq settled herself more onto the neck of the dragon that served as the headpiece for the ship. "Do you think," she inquired of the parrot, "that if we went straight in any given direction, we would eventually come across land?"

"Aye," Dante's voice answered softly beside her ear.

Jacq jumped; Bill flew up. "Really?" she asked, trying to look calm and not glare at his smiling face as he leaned lazily on the railing of the boat. "And why is that?"

"Why not? Everywhere leads to somewhere. It's just a question of where."

The two looked at each other in silence for a while. "You are, perhaps, very right," she admitted, sliding off the beam to stand in front of him.

"So, you really want to see the zebras of Africa?" he asked, crossing his arms as if greatly interested.

"Have you seen them?"

"Nay. I have not, lass." A strange silence ensued, beckoning them both to speak. However, neither was willing, so they just watched each other for several seconds until Dante finally broke. "Would you like to help me with something?" He pushed off of the railing and gestured the other direction.

"Of course," she agreed readily, speaking as if she'd been holding her breath. She trotted after him. "What do you need my assistance with?"

Smiling down at her, he responded, "You shall see."

"What?" Jacq laughed in disbelief at his denial of disclosure. "I agreed, but you're not going to tell me what I agreed to?"

His brow knotting at this, he looked skyward, then back down at her. Staring at him, she waited expectantly. Staring right back at her, he scratched the side of his nose, contemplating giving in, then, smiling, he chuckled. "Nay!"

As he strode off, Jacq's mouth fell open, and she stared after him for a short moment before breaking into a run and catching up to him in a few strides. The coins strewn all over her jingling musically, she spouted, "Wha-what? That's ridiculous!"

"You are the cabin girl," he reminded when she bound in front of him, forcing him to come to a halt.

"Just the cabin girl?" Jacq retorted playfully, batting her eyelashes just a little. "You do know our services are *strictly* a favor, as it is not at all our fault *you* left *your* cabin boys at the docks, savvy?" She smiled at him in unauthentic innocence.

Watching her, he did a horrible job of stopping himself from smiling. "Oh!" he snorted. "If you must know, you're going to help me mend a sail!" Pushing past her,

Dante began moving forward again, looking at her over his shoulder as she about-faced and hastened after him. The corner of his mouth remaining pulled up at the corner despite his efforts to have a straight face, he clasped his hands behind him and watched her fall into step beside him.

"What?" she sputtered, sounding baffled at his behavior. "What are you looking at me like that for?" After a few moments of silence, she added, "I want you to know, I very much dislike to sew."

"That's why I've chosen you to help me," he replied, continuing to keep his eyes straight ahead, his hands clasped behind him. She stared up at him as she continued to walk by his side, bumping into the sailors that she didn't see. "I dislike it as well," he admitted, a very pleased smile carving his mouth.

Watching from near the helm, Madam McLoflin fanned herself as she watched the two girls going about their own business—Alex keeping James company, Jacq lending a hand to the crewmen. Turning her back haughtily toward them, she gazed out across the waters and murmured, "Amy, darling, I'm so dreadfully sorry. When I get back to your father, I shall tell him of our absolutely horrible loss. Perhaps then he will become the man I have wished him to be for so many long years."

"I could be that man of fire that ye so desire," a man's voice floated up from behind her.

Spinning about sharply, Madam McLoflin came face to face with Viking Pierce, standing boldly before her, done up in his full Viking attire. "*Eek!*" she erupted, her hands jumping into the air in disgust. "You are such a

dreadful boy! You are an embarrassment to your proper place in society! Do you know what society has come to these days? Oh! It's dreadful! Horridly dreadful! We are to know everything and yet nothing all at once, you see," she lectured, shaking her finger at him. "But I see you are an expert at knowing nothing, least of all your proper place in society. I've seen you have a caretaker or butler or some kind, which would so suggest that you were of proper English breeding. And yet, here you are, standing so foolishly gallant in the clothes of savages of the past!" With that, she put her nose in the air, spun about, and marched down the nearest stairs and disappeared into her quarters.

Viking Pierce stood staring at where she'd been standing until the distinct *click* of her door broke his stunned state. He blinked several times, then, choosing his words rather deliberately, he muttered, "Mr. Bibbs, was it that bad?"

Mr. Bibbs, who was standing just a short ways off, took a good look at Viking Pierce. "I assure you, I did not think it was that poorly written, sir."

Nodding his head, Viking Pierce traipsed off, thoughtfully thinking aloud, "It took me nigh on half an hour to get it just so ..." Rolling his eyes, Mr. Bibbs sighed heavily, then trudged off after him.

Witnessing this small commotion, Jacq glanced across the sail at Dante, who, seeing her glance, was eyeing her suspiciously. Jacq snorted, picking up her needle and thread again. "She is an odd one, that Madam."

Shrugging, Dante eyed his stitching. "You don't trust her?" He looked up at her from under his eyebrows.

Jacq stopped short in her sewing, then, pulling the string rather deliberately, she returned smoothly, "Should

I?" Her voice dropped to a murmur. "After all, what has she done to give us reason to trust her...I mean..." She exhaled sorely.

Continuing in silence, Jacq's mind ranted on, *Of all the nonsense. Who does she think she is? She knows she lied. I know she knows she lied. She knows I know she knows she lied. So, why does she carry on as though her known secret is still safe with her? Perhaps she has lied to herself that she doesn't know she knows I know she knows she lied. Perhaps I shall go see if she has anything to say.*

"Jacq..." Dante's voice interrupted her.

"*What?*" she erupted, inhaling sharply as though she'd been caught red-handed doing something illegal. He stared at her. She exhaled slowly, forcing her breathing to regulate. "Aye, Dante?"

"Your sewing is both fast and efficient," he noted, waving at how far she'd come relative to where he'd reached.

Looking first at him in surprise, then down at her work, she was rather stunned at what she saw. Over half the sail sat piled on her right side. The needle in her right hand was still in midair, where it had stopped when Dante interrupted her thoughts. Turning to him, she smiled pleasantly, though awkwardly. "So it seems..."

"Perhaps you should go talk to her," he said, smiling at her knowingly.

Eyeing him, Jacq questioned, "Who?"

"Whoever it be that be keepin' yer mind out o' yer head, lass!" he snapped gruffly, winking at her. He added an insisting smile to encourage her to go take care of whatever was troubling her.

Smiling guiltily, she continued to sew a few more stitches, then sighed. "I do not wish to make her uncomfortable if she did not lie."

Turning his full attention to her, he looked her up and down, taking her in overall. Then, pensively, he replied, "I believe you, and I believe that you will be as proper as you should be."

Jacq froze. "You do?" She thought about Viking Pierce and that he could be leading these people that had become her friends to nothingness. *That's a first...*

The corner of his mouth lifted in a smirk, and his eyes read of amusement. "Aye," he returned easily.

Within a few moments, after Dante coaxed her a little more, Jacq found herself standing at the door to Madam McLoflin's room. Biting her lip, she took a deep breath, then knocked on the wooden barrier. Listening, she could hear the woman's feet scuffling toward her. Then she opened it, her red hair swaying with the motion, her cold, green eyes peering at Jacq.

The girl felt her right hand clench, and she suddenly envisioned herself punching the woman right in the middle of that skinny nose of hers. Surprised at this violent thought, Jacq jumped back, shaking her head.

"What's the matter?" Madam McLoflin sputtered. "Is there something in my hair?" She began frantically spot checking herself with her fingertips. "On my face! Oh! Dreadful! Rot! This ship is horridly unsanitary! Anything could be anywhere!"

After watching her crazily search herself, Jacq rolled her eyes and cleared her throat to answer. "Nay, Madam."

"Oh. What then? You wish to speak with me?" Her eyes drilled deep, but Jacq ignored them.

"Aye, Madam," she replied in a polite monotone.

"Oh, very well. Come in, come in." Stepping aside, she allowed Jacq through the door first and closed it behind them. "What did you wish to speak with me about? Is there something troubling you?"

"Aye," Jacq admitted, smiling to herself. "There is indeed."

Madam McLoflin crossed her arms uneasily under the gaze of the twin. "Well, what is it, dear? Your just standing there does not allow me to be of any use to you."

Jacq didn't move her eyes, and she didn't speak. She merely stood, wringing her fingers behind her, thinking, *You know I know. I can see it in your eyes, and you know it.*

"You think I lied to you!" the woman gasped after a few more moments of silence. Jacq neither spoke nor moved. "I don't see how you drew such a conclusion after I offered you all that I know. You know it's painful for me to remember such days," Madam McLoflin blubbered.

Keep talking, wench, Jacq thought. *An innocent soul of high society such as you would never have thought of lying unless there is something you wish to hide in a deep, dark corner.*

Her face flushing, Madam McLoflin's breathing quickened. She swallowed hard as she stared back at Jacq. "Truly," she broke, beads of sweat appearing across her forehead, "you don't think so lowly of me ...?" Her voice was coming in shriek-like whimpers now. "You have no way to prove your thoughts of me! No matter how much you dislike me!"

"Madam," Jacq whispered, "I have not said a word." *And yet I should spend many hours in repentance once I leave this room.*

Her lip trembling, Madam McLoflin sniveled, "Your mother and I were dear friends. We grew up together. We were as good as sisters to one another, vowing to take care of each other until the day the other died." At this, she sunk onto the bench beside the window. "And then..." She sniffled. "And then, I saw Bartholomew. He was the most handsome man I had ever seen, tall and strong. He was perfect... He had decent wealth, a good reputation, a name for himself, and he was looking to start a family."

She paused, hugging herself as her lip continued to tremble. "I took your mother by the harbor so she could see him and approve. She was immediately attracted to him, but being my friend, she mentioned it not and wished me the very best. The next time I went down to the dock in hopes he would speak to me, he did. But it was to ask your mother's name. He'd fallen in love with her without even knowing anything about her." She let go of her arms and began to wring her hands together in her lap.

"They were married in less than three fortnights, and a few years after that, she conceived. Oh, they were happy, with and without her pregnancy. I offered to be the governess." At this, Madam McLoflin raised her eyes to stare into those of Jacq's, which had softened but were no less intense. "Out of the love I had for your mother and our friendship over the years, I set aside my love for your father and agreed to be the governess," she repeated pointedly, emphasizing the words "love" and "governess."

"Then, while your father was away on business, it came time for your mother to give birth." Madam McLoflin's hands stopped moving. Her eyes glazed over. "I helped her with the deliveries, but it was too much for Mary, and ... she died ..." The redhead's eyes melted into pools of sorrow, deep and complicated. "She lasted long enough to name you both, and then she passed on. I kept the two of you, Alexandria and Jacqueline, awaiting your father's return." She began to fidget with the folds of her skirts. "A few months later, I received news that he would not be returning from the seas. I was devastated. So, to deal with my grief accordingly, I gave you both up." She paused to take a deep breath. "For adoption." Looking Jacq in the eye again, she hurriedly continued, "I told the adoption house that you should go together, that it would be right, but they would not listen. They were certain that nobody would want two children at once." Bursting into tears, the woman bawled, "Are you satisfied now?"

Jacq eyed her, the softness fading. "So who are you a governess for now?" she asked, clenching her molars together.

"Amy, the daughter of Mary's younger sister, Sarah," she said, staring out the window.

"So I have a cousin aboard a pirate ship?" Jacq inquired, her eyebrow peaking at this idea.

"Yes," Madam McLoflin responded awkwardly. She sat, pensively thinking a moment before she continued. "You do."

"Tell me," Jacq requested, her eyes softening as she sat down across from the fiery-haired woman, "what did my mother look like?"

Madam McLoflin turned in surprise and was pleased to see the girl's softened expression. "Why," she breathed, her eyes tearing up again, "she looked much like you and Alex. You have her face... and her smile." The woman touched Jacq's undone hair, which cascaded out from under her bandana. "But you have your father's eyes," she noted, staring deep into the hazel eyes Jacq possessed.

Nodding, Jacq smiled softly. "Thank you, Madam McLoflin. Sorry to have upset you."

"Oh." The woman breathed sharply. "Not at all, dear. You deserve to know the truth."

"Aye," Jacq agreed, moving toward the door. She bowed her head at the woman and then let herself out. As she shut the door, her pleasant smile turned into a scowl. "Wench," she muttered under her breath. Swallowing a lump in her throat, she walked away as casually as she could muster.

As Jacq shut the door, Madam McLoflin's eyes turned to flames. Her pretty mouth twisted into a snarl. "Don't interfere, whelp," she growled. Tossing her flaming red hair, she folded her arms and scowled up at the ceiling.

Just as she was about to descend the stairs to her room, Jacq felt someone grasp her arm, and she twisted around so violently that she fell right into his arms. Looking up, she saw Tom staring down. "Be ye feelin' well?" His eyes seemed larger than those of the dragon headpiece. Jacq shuddered, her jaw clenched. Tom touched her cheek and petted her hair. "Ye be needin' to calm yerself, lass," he whispered. "Breathe."

Jacq inhaled slowly. "She lied again," the twin whispered hoarsely. "There is something she won't tell me. Something that is very untrue about her story. I can feel it."

Tom swallowed hard. Then, putting his arm around her shoulders, he escorted her to her room. There, he insisted she lie down in her hammock. "Don't be thinkin' too hard, lass," he advised. Leaning over her, he gently placed his lips to her forehead.

At his touch, she closed her eyes and whispered, "Thank you, Tom."

He smiled sadly. "Ol' Tom knows best. Don't be thinkin' too hard."

Backing out of her room, he shut the door as softly as he could. Smiling to himself, he turned to go up the stairs and came face-to-face with Miata. "Ah!" He jumped back at the other man's silent approach. "Ye be scarin' ol' Tom!" He laughed uneasily.

A stern glare firmly formed Miata's usually panicky features. "Be watchin' yerself, Tom…" he warned. "I be tellin' ye she be off limits to ye. *If* one o' us were to be winnin' her, it surely wouldn't be ye!" Leaning forward, his eyes were more threatening than anything he could have possibly said.

Holding up his hands in surrender, Tom coughed up another awkward laugh. "If ye be insistin', mate… If ye be insistin'…"

Chapter 7

Swinging down from the rope ladder between the rail and the mast, Dante took a deep breath as he landed soundly on his feet.

"Yer like a cat, Skippy."

Dante looked over his shoulder as he straightened to find Tom whittling a piece of wood. "How do you figure?" He squinted in the morning light and crossed over to Tom's side.

As Dante sat down, Tom paused and explained, "Ye always be landin' on yer feet, no matter how high ye be fallin' from."

Still squinting, Dante looked at the crude piece of wood Tom held in his hand. "Have you tested this theory of yours?" Tom gave him a puzzled glance. "I mean, how do you know cats always land on their feet?"

"Skippy, ol' Tom's seen plenty o' cats be fallin' and then be landin' on their feet."

Nodding, Dante said, "Someday they're going to charge for that." He motioned to the piece of wood Tom held.

Tom's eyebrows knotted. "How be ye figurin' on that?"

Shrugging, the boatswain drummed his fingers on his leg. "They'd make a week's wages off of you in three days."

Tom smiled and the two laughed.

"Skippy."

"Aye?" Dante returned, closing his eyes at the sunlight and leaning back.

"Ye know who Jacq be remindin' me o'?"

Dante's right eyelid flew up and he moved to look at Tom better. "Who?"

"Guinevere. Be ye rememberin' her still?"

Dante's face clouded. "Tom..."

"Ol' Tom be thinkin' Guinevere were yer first, aye? She were afore Scarlet, Charlotte, an' Martha, the three sisters. An' afore Elizabeth, Rosalyn, an' Patricia. She were afore Victoria as well, aye? Victoria..." He sighed. "She always were one to be keepin' a secret." He chortled at this. "Ol' Tom be rememberin' all the others too, Skippy," he promised, sounding so pleased with his talent. "An' ye," he added, giving Dante a friendly punch in the shoulder as the man looked at him with an unsettled air, "ye ne'er had to pay a one! Nay! They was all wantin' to be with ye."

An uneasy smile played across Dante's lips.

"Ain't it so?" Tom asked, dissatisfied with his friend's reaction. "Damn Skippy...everyone knew ye by that name...Ye were one o' the best. One o' the most envied by lads, an' most sought after by lasses."

"Aye," Dante agreed, studying the grain of the wood next to him. "But all that has changed, Tom. I no longer sail under those colors."

Tom stopped his whittling and eyed the ex-buccaneer. "Ol' Tom be wonderin' if ye be able to completely change yer colors."

Slowly, Dante turned and observed his friend quietly go back to work on what now was a splinter. "If you whittle that piece of timber long enough, it will disappear," the boatswain pointed out. "I've been whittling for a while." His gaze turned to the sea. "Captain Taylor taught me many a lesson afore his death."

Nodding, Tom smiled and inquired quietly, "But be ye able to be withstandin' the temptations if they was to be presentin' themselves in a strong manner? They be sayin' a cat don't change his stripes ..."

"What are you talking about?"

Tom's eyes grew at his friend's angry expression. "Ol' Tom were just questionin' ye, mate. It be nothin' more."

Dante, continuing to glower, turned his gaze back to the sea. "Keeping company like yours is the closest I intend to be to crossing back over into those waters ..."

"Be she knowin'?"

"Be who knowin' what?" the boatswain snapped.

Clamping his mouth shut, Tom shook his head. "It be nothin' and nobody at all, Skippy. There be no question in ol' Tom's mind that be just dyin' to be gettin' out an' findin' an answer." Tom dropped his skinny little sliver and put his knife away.

Taking a deep breath, Dante exhaled. "And what is this question?"

"Ol' Tom just be wonderin' if the pretty lass be knowin' aboot yer past an' all the other lasses, an' yer mother an'

all?" The dark-haired young man smiled weakly as he waited for Dante's reply.

Shaking his head, Dante admitted, "If you're talking about Jacq, then no, she knows naught of my past, except that I sailed with Captain Taylor." Dante ran his tongue slowly between his lips, pensively staring far into the horizon. His black hair, sticking up in all directions, moved as leaves in a tree. His red shirt billowed about him, and other than his blinking and muscles in his face rippling from clenching his teeth, he did not move.

"Jacq!" Alex's voice called. Pinching her eyes shut, Jacq rolled over in her hammock and groaned.

"Jacq! Wake up! I think I figured out the next line!" Alex whispered in her sister's ear.

Jacq jolted up, falling out of the hammock and sprawling on the floor. Alex stared at her, her jaw clamping shut in apology. Smiling and squinting in the light, Jacq winced, clearing her throat, and asked, "What do you believe it to say?"

"Oh! Right!" Alex opened her locket. "I believe it to mean *True to the marker stay and it will lead ye.*"

Jacq stared at Alex for a few seconds. "What is the inscription in the locket?"

"Stay and it will lead ye, True to the marker," Alex read.

Shrugging and nodding, Jacq admitted, "Yours is much easier on the tongue to say. It matches the others." There were several moments of silence as Jacq sat on the ground, thinking to herself and waiting for her brain to

wake up. Then, sighing, she added, "I spoke with Madam McLoflin."

"And what did she say?" Alex moved in closer, her eyes searching Jacq's face for any indication of how the conversation went.

"She lied to us," Jacq spoke. "And then she lied to me again." Jacq's cheeks flushed pink in frustration, and she began to admire the wooden floor. "How awful is that? Why would a high-society woman do such a terrible thing? Whatever her secret is ... it must be very good ..."

Her mouth twisting in consternation, Alex turned her eyes to the floor as well. "I know not, sister."

Taking a deep, ragged breath through her nose, Jacq bit her lip. Opening her mouth and exhaling, she looked back at Alex. "We shall get it out of her eventually. To that, I shall vow." Jacq looked deep into her sister's eyes with resolution gleaming in her expression.

Alex nodded, then lurched forward and gave Jacq a hug, hauling her to her feet. "We shall find out about us what we need to know, whether that woman wants us to or not."

Grinning, Jacq gave her a quick squeeze then pushed back from Alex and laughed. "You almost sounded aggressive. You must be careful ... I might be wearing off on you ..."

Letting go of her twin, Alex sat on her own hammock, saying, "Aye. But *almost* is the key word in that sentence, not aggressive." She smiled innocently.

Shaking her head, Jacq laughed and went about readying herself to join the rest on the upper deck. As she did so, Alex inquired, "Have you ever worn a dress?"

"A dress?" Jacq repeated, turning to look at Alex as she tied on her bandana. "Aye. But why do you ask?"

Alex smiled, batting her eyelashes slightly. "Just making sure you know how to put one on." With that, Alex hurriedly exited the room. Frank, tilting his head, scampered out the door after her before it shut.

"And why is that so important?" Jacq called after Alex as she disappeared. However, the question came too late for an answer as she vanished from hearing distance. Grinning broader than she had in weeks, Jacq looked down at Bill, who had crawled out of somewhere, and was standing beneath her hammock, staring up at her. "Do you hear that, Big Beak Bill?" She laughed. "Alex wants to know if I know how to put a dress on... What could she possibly want to know *that* for? I bet there's a reason she ran out of the room before I could ask any questions... What do you think?" Bill nodded vigorously.

"We'll get it out of her," Jacq told him, holding out her hand for him to hop onto. "She can't keep it a secret forever..."

"Sisters!" Bill clucked, nodding his head.

Twisting her mouth in thought, Jacq sighed. "Sometimes you worry me."

"*Land ho!*" Mr. Thames's voice bellowed.

Blinking once, Jacq quickly straightened all the coins on her sash and bandana and then raced up to take a good look at the land they were approaching. Flying behind her, Bill squawked, annoyed at the commotion. As Jacq breathed in the crisp freshness of the open air, Alex grabbed her hand and pulled her to the rail. Miata squeezed up beside Jacq, and the three stared ahead.

Gazing fixedly at the distant landmass, Alex breathed in a long, deep breath and a smile like one when seeing someone who has been absent for a long time spread across her lips. "It is beautiful."

"How can ye be tellin' from here?" Miata questioned, the intensity of his stare increasing as he squinted into the distance.

Rolling her eyes, Jacq chuckled. "Of course it's lovely, Miata! It's land!" Throwing Alex a quick glance, she added, "We are closer than ever to our answers." Alex nodded.

Miata smiled over at Jacq, watching the sun glimmer in her hair and reflect off of her coins. "Soon ye shall be knowin', mate..." He put a caring hand on her shoulder.

Smiling back at him, Jacq reached up and grasped his hand. "Aye, mate... Soon we shall have some answers..."

A short distance away, his eyes tearing up, Viking Pierce murmured, "We have found the island of the treasure, mate. Me translation was right." Smiling blissfully, he leaned against Mr. Bibbs, who turned a rather disgusted expression in his direction.

"Captain," Jacq called, trying to remain calm and mature, "when do you believe we shall reach shore?"

Captain Turner turned to answer his stand-in cabin girl, only to find himself staring deep into the eyes of an overly calm but extremely tense young lady. Practically holding her breath, the excitement was steaming off of her; she reminded him of a little girl on her way to ride her very first pony. Smiling the softest smile Jacq had witnessed in the entire voyage, the Captain replied, "Very soon, Miss Jacqueline. Near nightfall. We shall go ashore and set up camp for the night. Then we shall search on the

morrow." Giving her a gentle pat on the cheek, he turned on his heel and walked away, straightening his face.

Giddily, Jacq gave Miata a hug, whispering, "Look what we have done, Miata! We are on the other side of the world. Across the seas!" Pulling away just enough to look up into his kind, panicky eyes, she paused for emphasis. "Thank you!" Giving him a small kiss on the side of his face, she then bounded away.

Alex and Miata stared after her. Trying to hide his delighted smile as he touched where her lips had pressed against him with his fingertips, Miata looked at Alex. Attempting to keep a straight face as well, the twin simply said, "That was most generous of her."

The two turned to the sea to watch the land approach. Yet, even in that moment, Miata's smile drifted away, and his heart felt heavy.

Jacq, flying away from the railing, went soaring about the ship, amazed by even the simplest components. She flitted between admiring the carved wood and the ruddy color of the railing. Quite suddenly, all the clouds disappeared from the skies. All aboard were drawn to the deck. Even Madam McLoflin, with her snide and scowling attitude, found herself stepping out into the glorious sunshine. As she stood, gazing about, she heard someone above her clear his throat.

"What is it?" she inquired, unable to hide the contentment she felt from the sun.

"It is lovely, isn't it?" Mr. Bibbs replied formally.

"Yes. I am afraid that girl," she gestured toward Jacq, who was sitting near the headpiece again, "has a disease."

"Perhaps," Mr. Bibbs acknowledged, smiling to himself, "but let us pray that they never find a cure." His eyes lifted from the top of Madam McLoflin's parasol to the girl at the front of the ship.

Taking in a deep breath, Jacq hopped down from her perch and began to wind through all the crewmen aboard the vessel, standing on tiptoe every so often and humming her customary song. She gazed about her as though looking for something. "And who be ye lookin' for?" Tom inquired as she passed him by.

"Dante," Jacq replied, unfazed by Tom's asking. "I would very much like to have a word with him, but I cannot find him among all these." She gestured at the biggest man aboard the vessel, who stood directly in her path.

At this, Tom's face clouded, and his expression fell under shadow. He watched her continue bobbing up and down in front of him, looking for Dante for a few moments before he decidedly clenched his teeth and grabbed her hand. "Come with ol' Tom. There be somethin' ol' Tom be needin' to be tellin' ye."

Her eyebrows knotted. "Of what necessity do you speak?"

"Come," he coaxed, pulling her down the stairs to the lower decks. He listened a few seconds, then, once he was convinced they were alone, he whispered hurriedly, "Now, ye be listenin' to what ol' Tom be havin' to say. Our mate, Skippy ... he be ... well, he be a pirate, lass."

Jacq stared at him in disbelief. "Dante? A pirate?" She laughed. "It cannot be ..."

"Oh, but it are, lass. Skippy be a notorious buccaneer. A might good one at that, ol' Tom might be addin'. He

be good with lasses, and with commandeerin', as ye might say." Jacq opened her mouth, but Tom put his finger to her lips, and, looking nervously about, continued, "He be a dangerous lad, lass. There be pirates followin' us. Ol' Tom be the one who told the good captain we be needin' to go ashore tonight for protection."

Jacq felt her breath catch in her chest and a strange heated sensation creep through her veins as her stomach felt queasy. "I know we are being followed by pirates." She shuddered, but said nothing more.

Tom blinked at this, but carried on. "Don't be lettin' yerself be gettin' caught in that trap o' his. He be like a spider, weavin' a web and catchin' his lasses that way." He paused, letting her consider what he just said.

Above them, clouds started rolling in from seemingly nowhere. They were vast and dark, with many tears to shed. Everyone looked about in utter confusion, but accepted the change as odd weather. Everyone, that is, except Alex. As soon as Jim, who had sidled up next to her to share in her joy at seeing land, pointed out the dark masses billowing across the open sky, her eyes darted about the ship for Jacq, but to no avail. "Jim," she breathed, "help me find Jacq ... Something has happened! I must find her!"

Below, Tom held Jacq tightly by the shoulders so she could not escape. Her teeth clenched in anger as her eyes grayed with tempestuous turmoil. "Lass, ol' Tom be wantin' to travel the world with ye. We could be seein' so many things together. Ol' Tom would be watchin' out for ye. Ol' Tom ..." He paused awkwardly, and she turned her pain-stricken face toward him, her eyes red and welling with tears that were gnawing at their restraints, her chest rising and falling with deliberate, measured breathing. "Be lovin' ye." With that, he pulled her into himself to kiss her with the all the passion he possessed.

Silent as a shadow, Dante sauntered down the stairs. Seeing them, however, and not noticing Jacq had managed to turn her cheek in time to evade the display of affection, the corner of his mouth twitched, and he turned his gaze to the ground. Then, turning on his heel, he vanished back up the stairs, as silent as though he'd never come.

Jacq pushed Tom back. "I'm sorry. I cannot do this." His eyes clouded intensely. "Not right now," she amended. "I have to think about all you have told me."

Pushing past him, she disappeared up the stairs. Her tears dropping as evenly as the raindrops around her, Jacq raced back to the quarters she shared with her sister, slipping on the saturated decks as she went. She was sure she ran into a variety of the sailors, who no longer had smiles sprawling across their faces. In fact, were they all glaring mockingly at her? Shying away from all of them, she continued to run to her room without stopping. Upon entering, she slammed the door shut and collapsed to her knees. Stifled sobs shook her body, and she crawled to the wall.

Seeing her sister darting across the deck, Alex left Jim's side and entered the room just seconds after her. Frank and Bill sat quietly on her bed, watching the soaking-wet girl across the room. Speechless, Alex pulled out the cloaks the Bumbleridges had given them and offered Jacq hers soundlessly. Taking it, Jacq wrapped herself up and gazed at her sister with big pools of emotional upheaval. Shaking her head and grabbing her sister into an embrace, Alex asked, "What happened?"

"We can trust no one now," Jacq managed to say through her chattering teeth. "No one at all…" She sniffled, gasping for air between teary shakes. "Lies…They all tell lies…" Rainwater collected in her bandana streamed down her face and joined the tears from her heart.

By nightfall, the storm had subsided enough to permit them ashore. All aboard the *Sea Dragon* hurried to land to set up camp and enjoy the feel of earth beneath their feet again. As everyone on board, except Madam McLoflin, went about gathering the necessary materials for constructing suitable, though mediocre, shelters, Jacq kept an eye on Dante. As much as she believed him to be good, Tom's words clung to her mind as spider webs. Each time her eyes came to rest on him, Tom's voice whispered in her head, *From Guinevere to Francine, and all those that be in between. They was likin' Skippy too much for their own good.* She saw the rose petals falling from between her fingers to land on the frothy sea. *For a great lady*, she heard Dante repeat. *A great lady*, she thought to herself. *Who were they for? Francine perhaps? Victoria? Guinevere?*

Meanwhile, Dante, rather than speak to her, kept looking out across the stormy waves. He avoided both her gaze and her company. Stumbling about with the others, he assisted in collecting bamboo, palm branches, and rocks. Occasionally, when she was not looking, he would steal a look at her. Yet, each time he did so, he immediately felt compelled to look away.

His uneasiness was giving him waking nightmares…He could hear her laugh and feel the beautiful sunshine that spread its wings across them when she did. Then he would hear a gunshot and see her fall deep into the sea. Shaking his head, he began grumbling to himself. "Tom? Really, Tom? Where's the rum when you need it?"

Tom appeared, holding a bottle out to him. Casting a distrusting glance at him, Dante muttered, "You're always here when I need you, eh?" as he took the bottle from Tom's fingers.

Tom shifted his weight from foot to foot. "Ol' Tom always be here for ye, Damn Skippy." He watched as Dante lifted the bottle to his lips and then glanced out across the cranky waters. It was black. There was nary a star in the sky, and the moon hid her face behind the clouds. Squinting into the darkness, he thought he could see, perhaps, a vessel looming in the distance. "No bloodshed," he whispered, returning his glance to Dante. "No bloodshed."

"Of course not!" Dante laughed, slapping Tom on the back and shoving the bottle back to him. "There is no need for that. And it's Skippy, remember? Just Skippy…"

Smiling sheepishly, Tom nodded. "Ye be right, Damn Skippy. Ye be right more often than ol' Tom. Ye be a cat, always be landin' on yer feet."

His eyes watering slightly, Dante clapped his hand onto Tom's neck and jaw. "Thank ye, Tom Thomas. Your words are filled with flattery. I only hope that you too are correct in this matter." Turning back to gaze out into the tempest, Dante exhaled a long, heavy breath and then hoisted his collection of sticks onto his broad shoulders. "And may we benefit from it richly."

Captain Turner, who included himself in the making of the shelters and not merely in the directing, noticed Madam McLoflin hugging a palm tree nearby, watching. Trudging over to her, he lifted his voice over the sound of the wind and asked, "What is the meaning of this?" He gestured to her and the tree.

Overhearing his booming voice, Jacq perked her ears in their direction. Madam McLoflin replied, "I demand my own shelter. I will not share quarters with anyone here."

Standing akimbo for a moment and glancing at the workers around him, the captain took a deep breath. "Very well." Madam McLoflin cast such a glance in Jacq's direction, one might think she had won a great victory. "Build it yourself then!" the captain bellowed in addition as he spun and marched away. An impish grin played across the face of the twin, and she bowed at Madam McLoflin from the waist. A small distance away, Mr. Bibbs smiled.

The rain stopped altogether now, and the drenched men looked about with wide eyes and wrinkled brows. Turning to Jacq, Alex touched her face and whispered, "Bless you, my sister. Bless you." Jacq smiled in return but turned a sharp eye to the waters.

Though the rain stopped and the wind died down, the clouds persisted, and the darkness continued. Even still, with the help of Jim and a young crewman, the twins finished the shelter for them and their pets. The group erected four more shelters for the men to share, and an overhang for Madam McLoflin to sit and scowl beneath. Dante and Jim were selected to keep first watch, and though nobody said why, everyone, even Madam McLoflin, knew it wasn't because of wild animals.

Chapter 8

Dawn rose early the next morning, painting the sky with the most magnificent shades of yellow and pink she had on her pallet. The waters below her held still in awe of the beauty she spread across the heavens. The clouds from the night before had been drawn back from the sky at the presence of the sun like theatrical curtains. All was quiet except the usual jungle noises and the horribly annoying sound of Viking Pierce's snoring. He, however, was the first to wake and breathe in the crisp, fresh air that filled the sky. The sweet scent of last night's rain was all he could sense. It was all around him, and he wallowed in it for several minutes.

When he opened his eyes, however, he was rather surprised to see a man standing over him. The tip of a blade touched his throat, and the man stood blocking the rising sun. Gasping, Viking Pierce opened his mouth, though unsure of what he was going to say.

"Ah!" the man warned softly, tapping his blade on Pierce's white throat. "Don't cry out." A gold and white smile glinted in the man's tanned face as he leaned closer to Viking Pierce. "That may not be such a good idea, matey." His eyes, cold as a clear, blue sky in the middle of winter, sparkled as he straightened. Retracting his blade, the pirate motioned, and Viking Pierce was gagged as two other men roughly lifted him off the ground and dragged him away.

Mr. Bibbs curled up tighter in his sleep, unstirred by the stealing of Pierce. The dust from the small scuffle settled unnoticed, and the air calmed entirely. Not a single bird made a note; not a creature seemed to move.

In their small shelter, Alex had begun to surface from her sleep when quite suddenly a loud voice boomed, "Ahoy, peaceful travelers!"

Alex sat up staring wildly about her. Jacq moved, but did not wake. Alex reached over and gave her sister a hard shove. Muttering indistinctly, Jacq snuggled further into her cloak, continuing to sleep. Rolling her eyes, Alex punched her twin in the shoulder. Wide-eyed, Jacq all but jumped to her feet. "What? I'm up!"

"Something's not right," Alex whispered. "There is a strange man in our camp."

"Ahoy!" the deep voice blared again. "Come forth you cod-headed do-gooders!"

At this, all of the huts that made up their camp toppled to the ground, proving that pirates had, in fact, taken over their site. Lined up along the shoreline was an odd collection of the *Sea Dragon*'s crew. Jacq made out Captain Turner, Viking Pierce, Madam McLoflin, a blond girl she'd never seen before, and an assortment of crewmen, including Jim. A tall man with massive, curling locks of dark brown hair, shrouded in both ragged and beautiful clothes, strutted around them, his rapier clinking at his side with every step he took. A collection of who she assumed to be his men stood off to one side, grinning about as though they had something to be proud of.

As he paced, he eyed the entirety of the camp, a satisfied smile forming on his tanned and slightly weathered face. Then, rather abruptly, he stopped and stared, open mouthed, at a small cluster of men. "Well, well! Damn Skippy? Be that you?" the pirate blurted, gawking at Dante, who was fidgeting at one side of the camp.

Dante turned to look at the man, a strange expression taking over as he squinted in the pirate's direction. "Brown Bill Burgess," Jacq heard Dante reply. Looking about, he went on to recognize, "Deadeye Thad, Sea Legs John, Little Tut. I heard you three had been caught a few months ago." They grinned sheepishly, shaking their heads. It was obvious they were both honored he knew them and embarrassed he'd heard of their near capture. Walking forward, he smiled at two men that stood side by side, one with red hair and the darkest of eyes, and the other with hair the color of midnight and eyes as blue as the sunlit sky. "Richard Roberts and Robert Richards," Skippy acknowledged. They smiled in appreciation of his recognition. Twisting back to Brown Bill, he noted, "It's been a while."

"Be that true." Brown Bill chuckled gleefully. "Haven't heard yor name in a while, says I. Black Tom didn't tell me he were working with you." The pirate, obviously captain of the miscreants, grinned in delight. Rubbing his hands together, he scanned the line of people he had kneeling in the sand, heads down, hands tied.

Dante, red faced, turned to Tom, who now stood beside him. "I thought you said you were finished with thievery." His dark eyes sparked, and he loomed above Tom as a lion does its prey before devouring it.

Black Tom smiled and swallowed a large, iron lump in his throat. "Skippy," he replied in a low tone, "ye be over reactin'. Yer career were stalled, and knowin' that, ol' Tom only be givin' ye a helpin' hand." Reaching out to touch Dante's shoulder, Black Tom was disappointed to find it was not there, and Dante stood, shoulder pulled away in disgust, looking down on him. "Ye be soft, eh?" Tom snapped.

"Nay." Dante bared his teeth. "But you shall wish I never got involved."

"Be he with us then?" Brown Bill called over, having finished looking over his prisoners.

Throwing one last glance at the taller man, Tom spun to look at the captain and bellowed, "Damn Skippy be joinin' us, Cap'n!" Dante's nostrils flared, his eyes narrowed into glowing slits, his hand on the hilt of his sword.

"But of course he be!" laughed the captain, oblivious to Skippy's near explosion. "Nobody can resist runnin' lines with Brown Bill Burgess!" Then, turning to his captive audience, the crew of the *Sea Dragon*, he explained, "Unbeknownst to you, we been followin' you. All we be wantin' is the treasure you be seekin'. That be all." He smiled eagerly, as though his words amended his actions and there should be an easy resolution for their situation. "But, in case you be unwillin' to hand it over freely, we confiscated some bargainin' chips, you might say." Gesturing toward the men and women along the shoreline, he then planted his feet shoulder-width apart, crossing his arms. "Be there any questions?"

Jacq sat smoldering amongst the pile that once made up their shabby hut. The two pirates behind her and Alex were whispering about them; she could hear it. Alex, sitting primly, tried to ignore them in her ladylike fashion. However, Jacq, finding she was not as couth and dignified as that, vaulted to her feet and blurted, "Do not speak so of my sister, or I shall use your own swords to silence you!" Standing defiantly between them and Alex, Jacq could feel all eyes focus in on her—not exactly what she had been going for.

Curiously, Brown Bill left his post and wandered over to his men for a closer look at the instigator of the commotion. He let his eye soak up her image for several seconds before motioning and turning back to return to his previous post. "Bring her."

"I will bring you no fortune!" she warned, evading their grasp. "But I can give you what you seek." Making eye contact with the pirate captain, she smiled a wild, devilish grin. He paused, looking back at her over his shoulder. "First, I wish to speak with the lass you hold hostage."

"Haha!" laughed the pirate. "What you ask cannot be!"

The corner of Jacq's mouthed turned up. "Then I shall ne'er tell you, and the secret shall die with me."

Marching up to her, the pirate asked, "An' what makes you so certain you can strike an accord with me, lass?"

Jacq swallowed anxiously while maintaining a calm exterior. "Without what I know, you shan't find that treasure."

Tilting his chin at this, he leaned forward and asked in a hushed tone, "You be only wantin' to speak with the lass? It be about no mischief?"

"Aye."

Holding out his hand, Brown Bill took a short breath, his face twitching as he waited for her to take his hand. "Then we have an accord." Alex grimaced as he touched Jacq's hand and then led her to the curling-haired blond by the sea.

Kneeling in front of her, Jacq cupped her hand about her chin. At her touch, the girl lifted her face, tear-stained and angry. Frowning at this, Jacq inquired softly, "What is your name, lass?"

"Amy Luray," the girl sniffed. "Who are you?" Her blue eyes were dark and tumultuous.

Blinking in surprise, Jacq replied, "I am Jacqueline Taylor Luray. I believe we are cousins."

Amy's brow furrowed. "That cannot be. My father has no brothers, and my mother has no sisters. You cannot be my cousin."

Jacq's narrowed eyes flashed to Madam McLoflin, who was shifting uneasily in the soft sand. Then, moving her gaze back to Amy, she whispered, "You will return home, I promise you." Jumping to her feet, Jacq cleared her throat. "I shall give you the last of the map, once you set these," she gestured to all those on their knees, "free."

"Don't do it, Miss Luray," Captain Turner advised. The pirate beside him kicked his ribs.

Jacq's eyes flared, but she simply turned and diplomatically concluded, "Mr. Burgess, let them go and I shall tell you what you wish to know."

"I think you be tellin' me what I be wantin' to know first, lass. Then I be willin' to let them go." His eyes flickered, watching her squirm under his pressure. Raising her chin into the air, she looked him in the eye, saying nothing. Pulling his blade from his sheath, he stomped over to Amy and threatened, "She be dyin' needlessly if you be not willin' to pass on yor secret we all wish to be hearin' as was our previous accord."

She felt the hit solidly in her gut. Her throat closing, she had to force herself to swallow her heart. However, to those watching, her composure still remained unaltered, despite his gesture. A silence cleared the air of any whispers that had been previously tossed about by the others on the beach. "Very well," Jacq sighed. Glancing at Alex, who was smiling softly at her twin, Jacq recited, *"Stay and it will lead ye, True to the marker / to set the treasure free, At last to dig in sand."*

"Be that all?" He pulled threateningly on the blonde girl's hair, wrenching a whimper from her.

"Aye ..." she said, keeping a cool, even look despite her insides growling fiercely at his gesture.

Pondering a moment, Brown Bill released his hold of Amy's hair, and then burst into laughter. "Of course!" Pulling out a compass from the sash about his thin waist, he declared, "We continue southwest until we see a marker. That marker will reveal to us the key and the spot of sand. Once we find that sand, we dig until we find the treasure! It be an easy chore, lads! That treasure will soon be ours!" In somber silence, Jacq listened to him rave, "Haha! Those old fools!" The other pirates cheered, brandishing their blades in the air.

It was then that Jacq's gaze fell upon Miata being patted on the back by Black Tom. As she fixed her sights on him, he turned to look at her. All the good things she had ever said about him, all the times she had ever stood up for him, withered into dust and blew away. A slithery, cold feeling wound its way around his throat and reached long, frigid fingers deep into his being to wrap around his heart and his stomach, choking him and making him feel weak and sick. He could not bear to hold the lock, and he let his gaze fall like a crumbling adobe wall, visibly shivering as though physically feeling the aftershock. Suddenly, all around him was quiet, and as she stared at him with her big, tear-glazed eyes, he heard her whimper, "You betrayed me…"

Miata felt sick, and he turned away, ripping both their gazes and her heart apart.

"Tie them up, lads!" Brown Bill roared to six men, including Black Tom, Skippy, and Miata. Turning to the rest of his men, he sounded, "To the treasure!" In unison, they fell in step behind Brown Bill and went thundering off into the Martinique jungle.

"You said we could go!" Jacq called after Burgess as two of the men advanced toward her.

"He said he be willin' to let ye go, but he ne'er said when nor where!" They laughed in a chorus.

"Ho there!" Mr. Bibbs called out to the crewmen. They stopped their groping for Jacq rather abruptly, spinning to face the Englishman. "I daresay! Why did you take my servant instead of me?" Gesturing with a blade he'd drawn from his side toward Viking Pierce, he crossed his arms in want of an explanation.

"Mr. Bibbs?" Jacq backed away from the buccaneers.

Chortling, the pirates offered, "We be willin' to tie ye up alongside him if ye be wantin'."

"Poppycock!" Mr. Bibbs laughed brazenly. "What childish prattle! Of course I do not wish for you to bind me, you insolent fool!" Their mouths falling open, the two pirates exchanged glances. At this, Bibbs turned his eye to Jacq. "However, I wish for you to let them go." With that, he arched his left hand well above his head while his right held his sword straight out and slanting downward toward the ground. His feet, heels together, toes out, were squarely beneath him. Bending his knees slightly, he bounced up and down a little, and then challenged, "*En garde!*"

Viking Pierce's eyes were bigger than ostrich eggs. "Oh, LORD, have mercy," he mumbled, staring at the positioning of his butler.

As everyone in the camp stared open-mouthed at Mr. Bibbs, Jacq sidled up beside Captain Turner as though to get a better view. The buccaneers, except Skippy and Miata, who were left on guard, lined up for their turn at the old man. As soon as Bibbs began to dance about, Jacq plucked away at the Captain's knot. When she had loosened it enough he could move his hands, she went on to the next most able-bodied crewman.

Viking Pierce was muttering, "Show them what for, old man!" under his breath.

When Black Tom approached Mr. Bibbs, a sneer on his face, he asked, "Shall ol' Tom be goin' easy on ye, old man?"

"Don't bother," Mr. Bibbs replied politely, "for I shan't go easy on you." He sneered at the young man. This gesture, in turn, boiling Tom's blood at the old man's challeng-

ing impudence in his direction. Thrusting his sword forward, Black Tom was surprised when Mr. Bibbs was suddenly beside his ear, whispering, "You shan't ever have her."

Pushing back from him, their blades ringing with the friction, Black Tom laughed. "Ye cannot be beatin' ol' Tom! Ol' Tom be one o' the best swordsmen e'er to be gracin' yer presence." Spinning, Black Tom stepped forward and sideways, then lunged forward, barely missing Mr. Bibbs's coat.

"Even if you were the better swordsman," Mr. Bibbs carried on, doing some fancy sidestepping of his own, "what makes you believe you shall win her heart?"

"*Ha!*" Black Tom gasped, tossing aside Mr. Bibbs' strike. "Every lad be havin' his price. Ol' Tom shall be rich soon enough." The air rang with the sound of their swords clashing and the cheering of the pirates on Tom's behalf.

Swinging diagonally down, Mr. Bibbs retorted, "Not only are we speaking of a lady, not a lad, but we are speaking of her heart, which never can be truly bought." With that, he bore his weight against Black Tom, knocking him back. He glanced at Dante.

Seeing his glance, Black Tom sprang away from the tiring man and threw his arm about Dante's neck. Everyone froze in surprise as Black Tom tightened his hold on the man's throat.

Jacq, who was nearly finished untying the second to last man, blurted, "Tom! What are you doing?"

His eyes, wild with adrenaline, stared at her. "Ol' Tom be wantin' ye to come with him. Ol' Tom be wantin' ye to travel the world with him. Ol' Tom can put the world at yer fingertips, Jacq."

Jacq's eyes moved from Black Tom to Alex. She glanced from Alex to Amy to Mr. Bibbs to Captain Turner to the sea and then to Dante—all the while, her mind buzzing at the awkward position Tom was putting her in. Tightening his grip on Dante, Tom's eyes blazed. "Ol' Tom be demandin' ye to choose."

Suddenly the sky became overcast. Jacq's mind blurred into images of Alex, Dante, Miata, and everyone smiling, and she felt nauseous. She remembered the Bumbleridges and Captain Taylor. She saw her world stretching out, vast, before her. The unanswered questions for Madam McLoflin whispered in her ear. Questions about her past... Questions for her future... The thumping of her heart muscling out the whispers, she stared at Tom and Dante a few brief moments when a seductive smile played across her lips. He *had* been ever so honest with her about Dante and Dante's piratical ways.

Both Tom and Dante blinked in surprise. "Tom," her voice began, sweet and melodious, yet sad and somewhat distant, "do you think it's really a choice?" She took a step forward. "Do you really think I have to choose?" The entire camp was inclining their ears and turning their full attention to the escalating scene Tom had created.

Releasing Dante, who dropped to the ground, coughing and holding his throat, Black Tom smiled as Jacq came closer, seemingly drawn by a magnetic force. "Go ahead and kill them all. I've never wanted anyone," her eyes shifted from Tom to Dante, her breathing forcibly regulated, "but you."

Glancing up, Dante barely caught her eyes before flicking back to Tom, who was so drunk with her words he hadn't noticed.

"No!" Alex cried, jumping to her feet and hurrying toward her sister.

Black Tom stuck out his arm, hitting her in the face. She fell to the ground, a dull thud resounding as she hit the sands. Alarmed, Jacq stopped dead in her tracks.

Miata's eyes widened as a small stream of blood trickled from Alex's lip. Drawing his pistol, Miata muttered, "I said no bloodshed."

Black Tom drew his firearm, pointing it at the young thief and glancing down at Alex, who was now wiping her mouth. "It were an unfortunate mistake."

"One that be not happenin' again!" Miata shouted, pointing at Black Tom, shaking at the mere fact that he was actually holding a gun, let alone pointing it at someone.

Cocking his head to one side, Black Tom grinned, his eyes glinting eerily. "Don't be bein' a fool, mate … Ye can't be doin' it."

Defiantly, Miata forced the pistol level with Black Tom's left shoulder and held it there. In response, Black Tom bore into the lad with such a look as no one has ever been able to reduplicate. Miata trembled. Black Tom raised his own gun and took deliberate aim at the young man. A malicious sneer creased his lips. His long thumb reached up and pulled down slowly on the hammer. Black Tom sighed. "Ol' Tom were tellin' ye, ye can't be doin' it."

Kawack! The deafening sound echoed, causing all nearby to shudder and fall silent. Dante, who had finally regained his breathing and color, sat up, looking between

Black Tom and Jacq. Miata fell to his knees and stared at them. Jacq, her eyes brimming with tears, stood tall, her lower lip trembling. Black Tom dropped his pistol and fell to his knees, touching the growing red, damp spot on his shirt. Swallowing, Jacq looked down at the smoking firearm in her hand, a growing queasiness taking hold on her. "But I can."

As Tom exhaled his last and fell to the light colored sands, one of the pirates knocked her over backward, sending the entire camp into an all-out brawl. The prisoners along the shoreline whose bonds had been loosened sprang from the sands and rushed in to help the rest overtake their momentary captors. Red Rob and Red Rich dropped to their knees and began flinging lead in every direction possible.

As Jacq pushed herself into a sitting position, she heard a loud crack and almost immediately thereafter felt a sharp pain in her shoulder, severe and unforgiving. Yelping, she fell back to the sandy beach floor, hitting her head hard when she did. At the sound of her cry, Dante winced and shuddered but then leapt into action, running, Jacq thought, in slow motion, to defend Captain Turner's back. Grinding her teeth in anguish, she wished she could simply disappear.

Out of the corner of her eye, she saw Jim and Captain Turner attack the lead-slinging duo, brandishing their blades like wild men. Hopping to their feet, the two accepted the challenge, drawing their swords. Alex was coming to tend to Jacq, but Jim somehow managed to let Red Rob take a good stab at him, and he fell. Crying out,

Alex veered from her trek to Jacq and flung herself at Jim's fallen body.

Jacq's mind swam in muddled pools of memory. She could hear Tom's voice, she could see Dante's face, and she could feel the strong arms of Captain Taylor holding her tight and whispering that it would be all right. If she just held on, all would be well again. She felt cold and could feel her breathing growing shallow. Amidst all the chaos, she could hear Captain Turner's deep voice, calm and sure, strong and gentle, in her mind say, "Fear not, lass. Sometimes angels fall. The trick to life is to get back up again." Then, her eyes blinked shut.

All fell silent in the camp again as the remaining three pirates, for neither Skippy nor Miata had fought on the side of the buccaneers, were gagged and secured to a tree nearby. The few wounded were being tended to by others in the crew as Captain Turner meandered about the camp, double checking the roll.

"Shall we go after the others?" Viking Pierce inquired of the captain as Mr. Bibbs knelt to untie him. Glancing at his butler, he then muttered, "And wherever did you learn to fight like that?"

Her eyelids flying open, Jacq found herself being examined by the ship's physician. She gasped in pain, but then grit her teeth to prevent another from escaping her lungs. "She's awake!" he called out.

Hearing this, Bibbs quickly crossed over to where she lay propped against a tree, Miata slinking a small distance behind him to avoid being seen by Jacq. "Nay. Don't go after them ... What we seek is not here." Forcing herself up, she whispered, "We must board the *Sea Dragon* at once."

"There, there, dear girl..." Supporting her as she struggled to push herself up, Mr. Bibbs nodded and turned, yelling out her instructions.

Everyone turned their eyes to her. She looked about, seeing that Dante, Miata, and Madam McLoflin had their hands bound and were under close crew supervision. Alex was still absorbed with tending to Jim's wound, and she realized she suddenly felt very weak and very alone. Her eyes became listless, and she felt her mouth moving but was uncertain of what she was saying. "We...We must board the *Sea Dragon*. The pirates...The pirates cannot follow. We must...must return to Port de Couler de Bateaux. Don't let them follow...Board the ship..."

Scooping the young woman into his arms as her knees buckled, he caught her just as she toppled over. "Captain," he advised, "let us depart immediately, and bring them with." He gestured toward the trio of questionable loyalty that remained bound together.

Giving one nod as an answer, Captain Turner waved his hand, and the crew moved back toward the ship. "Mr. Rackham," the captain murmured as the man walked past. Dante stopped, head up, and waited. "Mr. Rackham, I like to think of myself as a man who knows the men closest to him."

"Aye, Captain." His jaw clenched and his eyes fought from looking at the ground.

"Well, you were more honest with me than I thought—telling me your past, including all your transgressions." Dante said nothing, though his jaw continued clenching in tension. "So, to prove to me you had as much to do with those pirates as I think you did, you have two assignments."

Dante's eyes shifted down to the captain's. "Get rid of that ship." He motioned to the gray-brown vessel anchored to the far right of the small bay. "And return to the *Sea Dragon* so that you may be my first mate until Mr. Monroe recovers."

Picking up Dante's wrists, Captain Turner cut the boatswain's bonds and looked him in the eye.

A smirk pushing up the corner of his mouth, Dante said, "Aye-aye, Captain," and bounded away to attend to Burgess's ship, the *Avenger.*

Chapter 9

Meanwhile, across the island, Captain Burgess and his men had come across an old, metal cross shoved deep in the earth. Chiseled on it were further instructions Burgess interpreted to say to find the key in the crevice of the large rock nearby and to dig in the sand surrounding the marker. Even though no key had yet been unearthed, his men were slaving away at a hole when suddenly one of them struck something, causing them all to lay into digging even more. Dirt flew into the blue air, layering anything within a ten-foot radius of the hole with dust. As they worked, they sang:

> *There be many a thing in the world to see,*
> *Lasses and gold be two of the three,*
> *And a bottle of rum the other one be!*
> *Yo ho! A jolly good day 'twill be,*
> *When we get not one, not two, but three!*
> *Golden hair and eyes so fine,*
> *Such a pretty coin I want as mine,*
> *To keep and to buy a bottle of rum and a lass divine!*

Yo ho! A jolly good day 'twill be,
When we get not one, not two, but three!
Red lips so fair and so bright,
A lass to have by your side for a night,
To keep your money and your rum, woo with all
your might!
Yo ho! A jolly good day 'twill be,
When we get not one, not two, but three!
A taste on your tongue to savor,
Rum, says I, be havin' the sweetest o' flavor,
To make such a bargain for a bottle, a lass, an' his
gold, none be braver!
Yo ho! A jolly good day 'twill be,
When we get not one, not two, but three!

As they finally finished uncovering their find—a large chest, they cheered delightedly. Too impatient to wait to find the key, Burgess yelled, "Step away, lads! We'll get this bloody chest open!" Taking careful aim at the lock that held the heavy box shut, Brown Bill let a war cry ring out, echoed then by his men in a chorus that rather sounded like howling. Firing the shot, all fell silent, and they held their breath as Brown Bill shoved on the lid to see if he could reveal the much-coveted contents of the chest.

When he pushed the strongbox open, a large cloud of dust sprang into the air as the lid hit the powdery soil. All the men began coughing and had to wait for the air to clear again before they saw what lay inside. Crowding around, ready to pluck out as much of everyone's share as possible, they suddenly stopped. The hungry, gaping expressions on their faces dwindled away. What was this? Rocks? There was a piece of parchment and a small leather pouch nestled amongst the stones.

Picking up the leaflet, Burgess opened it and, glancing about at his disenchanted crew, pursed his lips and read, *"For he who was fool enough to find this here, ye be receivin' naught but the devil's share."* Plucking the leather pouch from its place, Brown Bill opened it, emptying the contents into his palm. "Six bloody coins?" he blurted, the veins in his neck and forehead standing out.

At his fiery tone, a loud boom resounded, and the lot turned to see a column of smoke rising in the distance. Looking up, barely able to see through the foliage, Brown Bill murmured, "By thunder... Lads! Go check on our bloody ship!"

For a moment they hesitated, wanting to demand an answer for what lay inside the treasure chest. However, turning on them in all his potential anger, Brown Bill shouted, *"Don't just stand here! Get a move on, ya addled whelps afore I shoot all o' ye!"*

In one tide, the thieves turned from their shovels and scampered toward the sea. Their captain remained at the excavation site, looking between the parchment and the coins. Thundering through the jungle, his minions quickly reached the sandy beach to find, not only one of the cohorts dead, but two missing and three tied to various palm trees. Away to their left, a huge fire burned, throwing agile flames into the air as though to flip through a trapeze routine. It was beautifully bright oranges and yellows, dancing high into the midday sky. Smoke billowed from its groping fingertips, blocking out the clear, blue sky and the horizon.

The heat of the massive inferno was so great that even the men who had just arrived at the scene were exhausted of their energy. The glorious blaze was emitting its beauty from atop the open waters, turning their ship into charred stubs that would never again be fit for sail. There was also, much to their dismay, no sign of the other vessel or those they had followed to this island in the Caribbean. In silence, down they sat, one or two at a time, on the sands of their coveted shore.

Watching the smoke fill the sky, Brown Bill Burgess sucked glumly on his lower lip. Pensively, he stared at the measly six coins he had journeyed all this way to uncover. "Black Fred and Gold Jem. Ye was said to be the most elusive pirate couple e'er to sail the seven seas. Now I be wonderin' if all yor stories be true. Bein' the only shipmate left alive after all our schemes, I thought I were bound to get yor treasure. Yet, here I be, just where ye knew I was to be, 'cause o' those two wenches ye bargained for to be keepin' yorselves company."

Wetting his lips, he dropped himself onto the soft earth and quietly watched the dust settle. "May yor luck soon be wearin' off on them and their kin."

Watching closely, Alex pursed her lips in want of asking a question as Amy brushed her curling hair. She opened her mouth several times, but nothing seemed suitable enough to emerge in sentence format. "I cannot," Amy finally spoke, "answer any questions you have."

Nodding, Alex said, "Aye, that I know." She hung her head, studying the floor of their room. Her brow contorted several times, directly reflecting her confused thought process.

Amy, a rather pretty girl herself, comparatively similar to the twins in size and stature, watched Alex in silence. Her cool eyes soaked in the older girl before her. She searched Alex for some kind of sign, but found none that she was looking for. Tilting her head to one side, she commented, "But, perhaps I know someone who can."

Lifting her head at this, Alex smiled, and her eyes danced. She had been trying to balance her time between Jim, Jacq, and this girl, attempting to build a rapport with her through their mutual experiences. It seemed her time had finally paid off. "Might I know this person as well?"

Smiling, Amy nodded confidently. "Yes. Perhaps you might, though not as well as you might suppose."

Gingerly reaching out and clasping the younger girl's hand, Alex's quiet smile transformed into a radiant grin. Starting at this, Amy took in Alex's expression and returned the firm grip.

"Bless you, Miss Amy," Alex whispered. "Bless you."

"Well, don't thank me just yet, Miss Alex…" Rising to her feet and straightening her mended dress, Amy led Alex out of the room and down into the lower deck. There, in two holding cells, sat Madam McLoflin and Miata. Here, the two young women stopped. Madam McLoflin raised her poisonous green eyes in an instant, only to flush at seeing Amy beside Alex. "Good day, Miss Amy," the redhead muttered, looking away.

"Good day, Margaret," Amy replied. Alex's eyes grew at this lack of title. "I wish for you to tell me all you know of Miss Alexandria and her sister, Miss Jacqueline."

Madam McLoflin wagged her head back and forth pitifully. "What do you wish to know, Miss Amy? If I had it my way, you would never consort with them." Her whole essence seemed to catch fire as she spat her words, beginning with her red hair.

"Margaret! I never! How could you say such dreadful things? They have been nothing but kind, and they have saved our lives. What are you keeping from us?" Amy's eyes sparked, and Alex suddenly saw Jacq standing there instead of Amy, her head held high and titled downward in disgust. Blinking in shock, Alex looked away.

From his dreary corner, Miata mumbled, "Go ahead and tell 'em, *Madam* McLoflin. Tell 'em what they be wishin' to know, or I will." He rose and walked forward, tall and shining like a star, his dark brown hair pushed back, a small mustache newly adorning his upper lip giving him a uniquely distinct presence.

"You know nothing!" she shouted hoarsely, turning to sneak a glare at him. Her eyes narrowed, the hair on the nape of her neck stood on end, and she brandished the most horrible sneer Miata swore he had ever seen.

Yet, sparkling like a new diamond in the first sunshine of spring, Miata smiled brilliantly and noted, "Ye be speakin' very clear English when ye be sleepin'…"

Her growling stopped. Clutching her throat, Madam Margaret McLoflin, gasping, stared dumbfounded at the young man and her skin paled. Tears streaming down her face, the broken tigress turned to the stunned girls on the other side of her cage. "Miss Amy," her timid voice mumbled, "you know you are the daughter of Sir Bartholomew Luray and the late Madam Elizabeth Luray." Amy nodded. Hanging her head, Margaret continued, "But what you do not know, child, what no one except me knows, is that Sir Bartholomew Luray and the late Madam Mary Luray successfully gave birth eighteen years ago."

Alex's lips parted in doleful anticipation. Covering her mouth with her hand, she somehow managed to turn the wail in her heart into silent anxiety and apprehensive anticipation.

"To twin daughters who Madam Mary Luray named Alexandria Luray and Jacqueline Luray."

Miata blinked, obviously as shocked with the woman's confession as both Alex and Amy. They watched as what remained of Madam McLoflin melted away in body-racking sobs. Margaret was regaining control of the fiery-haired woman, ever so reluctantly. Her haughty air diminished, and, as it did, she continued, "Sir Luray was away on a voyage, and dear Mary only lived long enough to breathe their names. I've been in love with Bart since the day I met him, so terribly long ago. And how I have dreamed of calling him Bart to his face ..."

She seemed to slip into the past as she spoke, her words sliding easily off her tongue. "Now, when Mary died, I thought that, maybe, if I gave away the children, then Bart would turn to me. But he did not." Pausing, she hung her head in defeat. "He married Elizabeth instead, and made sure he was present for the birth. He knew of his third child, and because his wife died, he held on to

Miss Amy dearly as the memory of all those he thought were dead."

Stopping, Margaret stared far away to some distant place. "He never loved me. I threw away three chances at a happy life for a man who will never love me in return." Exchanging glances, Alex and Amy then looked at Miata, their eyes teary and brimming with emotion.

"That be an awful rotten thing to be doin' to someone ye be claimin' to be lovin'," he said in a low mumble. Sitting back against the wall, he pulled a gold coin—the same kind Jacq had decorating her attire—from his pocket and began turning it over and over in his fingers.

Amy watched him curiously, Miata oblivious to her stare. "A rotten thing to be doin'…" He held back tears pushing on the backs of his eyes as he recalled the way Jacq had looked at him that day on the beach. Had he managed to kill the only true friendship he had ever known? Eternally separated himself from the girl he loved more than anyone else in his life? The idea…the realization…choked him.

Up above them, in Madam McLoflin's former quarters, Jacq sat on the cushioned bench by the window, peering out at the wake the *Sea Dragon* was leaving behind them. Her left arm, from her shoulder to her elbow, was wrapped against her body with white linens. Sitting on her knee, Bill nosed at the fingers of her left hand, which lay cupped in her lap.

"How does it feel?" Dante's voice broke the stillness as he stood in the propped open doorway.

Continuing to gaze trancelike out the portal, Jacq replied flatly, "It hurts when someone touches it, when I move it, and when I laugh."

Glancing out at the partly cloudy sky, Dante frowned at her distant tone. "I haven't heard you laugh in nearly a fortnight." Clasping his hands behind his back, Dante tilted his head and eyed her.

Swallowing an iron lump, Jacq blinked a moment then reiterated, "It hurts to laugh." Feeling his gaze on her, she fought against the desire to return the stare. Despite her efforts, she lost. Glancing at him, she then averted her eyes to the floor. "And I have been ill for much of the voyage back thus far."

"Aye," the young man agreed. "That you have been, lass. Very ill. We're lucky you pulled through. It was close for a while."

"Luck," she repeated. "Is there such a thing as luck?"

Observing her quietly for a moment, Dante sighed heavily, but silently, and turned on his heel. Seeing the shadow of him passing through the entryway, Jacq muttered, "You never told me you were a pirate."

Remaining in the doorway, his hand on the doorpost, Dante ran his fingers through his hair, running his tongue along his lower lip as he considered her comment. "You never asked ... And, frankly, it's one of those things one doesn't bring up unprovoked in a pleasant conversation."

Allowing herself to stare at his back, Jacq tried to think of something else to say, but she could find nothing. Curious, the temporary first mate spun about, catching

her gaze as she quickly relocated it to the sea beyond the window. Re-entering and closing the door, he took three careful steps to the center of the room. "Honestly, I can't believe you shot Tom."

She said nothing.

"I was a pirate, and I never shot anyone. Well, not fatally, anyway..."

Frank, who'd been dozing on the bed, hopped off and wandered toward Dante.

Jacq's brow furrowed, and she glanced at him over her shoulder. "What of all your lasses?"

"There was never really anything between us."

Reaching up to Dante's knee, Frank pulled lightly on his trousers.

"Then what great lady were those rose petals for?" Jacq snapped. She turned fully about to look at him squarely. Startled, Frank ran back to the bed, and Bill flew to the rafters.

Running his tongue over his lower lip again and crossing his arms over his chest, Dante stared at Jacq, studying her face. In his mind, he could hear her dreamy voice say, *I've never wanted anyone but you.*

Her heart raced as she watched him, shifting his weight from one foot to the other, his handsome face drawn with thought.

"The petals," he began gingerly, still fidgeting, "were for a great lady." Jacq's heart stopped; she felt her breath escape and not return. Eyeing her carefully, he continued, "They were for my mother."

At his words, she felt her throat swell and her heart burst. A rush of air filled her lungs. "Your mother?" she repeated, coughing a little and wincing from the pain the jarring motion inflicted on her. Her statuesque façade cracked. "I'm so sorry," she whispered.

Sitting at the opposite end of the bench, Dante sighed. "You have nothing to apologize for." He glanced out the window, cheek clenching. Jacq imagined she could hear his teeth grinding together. "However, I would like to extend my sincerest apologies to you, Miss Jacqueline."

Tilting her head at the top of her svelte throat at this use of her entire first name and title, Jacq waited apprehensively for what he would say next.

"It must have," he fumbled, "been difficult for you to put a bullet in the one man you loved."

A smile breaking her face, Jacq made both a gasping noise and a laughing noise. "Wha—Tom? He was merely a mate, nothing more…And he betrayed practically everyone I care about and got one of my best mates into a heap of trouble…"

Dante's eyebrow shot up at this, his mouth opening and closing in confusion as he tried to sort his thoughts. "Then…Then why did you kiss him?"

Her smile dropped in disgust. "I didn't kiss him—"

"I saw you!"

She felt a stone drop into the pit of her stomach. The moment she turned her head away to avoid Tom's advances replayed dreadfully in her mind. A silence eddied about them, filling the room with a cold, awkward stillness. If Dante truly believed this, she knew now that she was alone, drifting on a current to be abandoned on some hapless bank with life's other unwanted things. Her chest felt heavy and her head hurt from the stressful tone

of the idea at hand. Her hands felt cold and sticky, but her heart was racing. Her shoulder began to ache, and the pain pushed on the tears that were already pricking at her eyes.

Dante watched as a tear rolled down her cheek and dropped silently into her hand, which still lay open in her lap. "You may not believe me," she murmured. Dante's gaze fell to the floor, and he rose to his feet. Feeling her heart beating in her throat, Jacq found it difficult to speak. "But," she barely continued. Dante returned his eyes to her as she lifted hers to lock their stares. "He did *not* kiss me."

"Miss Jacqueline," Mr. Bibbs's voice interrupted, accompanied by a short knock on the door, "your sister wishes to speak with you, and it is time you get back in bed."

Beseechingly, she turned to Dante, who was walking agreeably toward the door. A heavy weight fell on her heart. *Why?* she thought to herself. *One mistake, and I am left with none but Alex, who has Jim.*

Fighting to maintain strong control over her emotions, a callous feeling crept over her spirit as she fought to not allow the severe disappointment to take hold of her. Outside, the winds began to blow in dark clouds nobody had seen on the horizon. A few large drops fell here and there on the deck.

At the door, Dante turned back. "Perhaps we shall speak again when we both find ourselves with naught to do," he suggested, "Jacq."

The clouds outside dissipated in a quarter of the time it had taken them to arrive. The yolk of sorrow she had all at once acquired disintegrated into little more than ashes about her feet. Lifting her face, she replied in a low voice she was barely able to maintain, "Aye, Dante. Perhaps we shall."

Outside, Alex, rather instantaneously, found herself bathed in warm sunlight, more splendid than anything they had seen in months. The days whispering of autumn's cold had been settling in, but this, this was marvelous. The *Sea Dragon* glittered like gold in the luminous sunshine. She smiled at the cabin door as Dante exited. He grinned sheepishly at the twin and gestured for her to please visit her sister. Breathing in a deep sigh, Alex hugged the tall sailor, then rushed past Mr. Bibbs and into the room.

Exchanging glances with Mr. Bibbs, Dante shook his head and walked away, muttering, "I'm glad she's feeling better." Mr. Bibbs just smiled, clasped his hands, and seated himself on a barrel beside the door.

While Alex relayed the information they had gotten from Margaret, Amy sat down below, watching Miata skeptically. The young man, being aware of it, paced back and forth. *What is she lookin' at? Maybe she be knowin' something about me that I don't be knowin'... What if... oh no... what if she be thinkin' she be knowin' something but really not? What good can be comin' o' this torture?* Beads of perspiration formed on his brow, and he was certain he was more nervous than he had ever been before in his life—which was quite a feat.

Finally, after what seemed to him like five hours, but had in fact only been about three minutes, Miata

inquired in a soft, almost hissing tone of voice, "Please, miss ... What is it that ye be wantin'?"

Amy glanced at Margaret, who, sodden in her own sorrows, was curled in the darkest corner of her cell. The blond girl traced the bars of his cell with her fingertips, and a half smile formed on her face. "Are you really what they say you are?" she asked in a hushed tone.

Leaning on the cage, Miata took a silent, deep breath. "What be they sayin' I be?"

Continuing to run her fingertips along the bars, Amy looked up at him from under her long lashes. "It has been said that you are naught but a common thief. They do not know what to do with you, since you betrayed your friends."

His heart sank a little at her words. Her big blue eyes engulfed him, and he fumbled for a few moments as he searched for a non-incriminating way to answer such an inquisition. "Aye, that be one way to be summin' it up," he found himself saying. Jacq suddenly appeared in his mind. "I've stolen a few things in me time, intentionally, but I were ne'er intendin' to hurt me mates. And I be intendin' ne'er to steal again." He watched her continue to watch him. "What of ye, lass?"

Amy leaned forward and held his gaze with a straight stare. "I am considered one of the finest-bred young women of my social class. I have never stolen anything except flowers from the garden." Her eyes moved up and down his face and upper body. "And I believe you."

His eyebrow arching, Miata returned, "And, exactly what age be ye, lass?"

"Sixteen." She smiled. "You?"

Moving his bottom jaw back and forth in thought, Miata simply replied, "Older than ye."

Smiling, Amy tossed her hair over her shoulder and sighed. "Heavenly." Then turning on her heel, she marched away, leaving a rather confused Miata still clinging to the bars of his cell.

Chapter 10

"Land ho!" Mr. Thames's voice rang out in the earlier hours of a morning a few weeks later. Jacq, whose arm was now mobile, and Alex, who were fixing net by request of Dante, stood up excitedly. Amy appeared from below, her body vibrating with zeal. Viking Pierce burst into tears and hugged Mr. Bibbs, who didn't take notice as he watched the twins thoughtfully.

"The time has come," he noted in his prim English voice, "for amends."

Releasing his grip, Viking Pierce stared up at his butler. "I apologize for not being aware of your battle capabilities," he spoke sincerely in perfect, high-society English.

Mr. Bibbs turned an arched eyebrow on Viking Pierce. "Thank you, sir." The two eyed each other a moment. "Pardon me for a moment, sir. I shall return in but a few moments." As Pierce nodded, Bibbs moved off, hands clasped behind him, down the stairs toward the girls.

Approaching the twins, Mr. Bibbs cleared his throat. "Excuse me, girls. I just believe that it is time you both made your amends. It has been a long voyage, and I believe there is some forgiveness to be given and received amongst many of those aboard this vessel." He watched them with his sincere, gray eyes, wanting to read their responses before hearing them.

After a few seconds of thoughtful silence, Jacq nodded. "There is someone that I must speak with. Pardon me," she requested, pushing herself up and brushing by the butler.

As Alex and Bibbs watched her walk away, the two twisted and asked, "Dante?" "Amy?" in unison. Shrugging, they turned back again, only to find they could not see her.

Disappearing downstairs into the lower decks of the ship, Jacq listened to her coins jingle over the din above her. Walking mindlessly down the corridor she had entered, she stopped in front of a lanky young man feeding Bill. "There you are." Sighing, she leaned against the bars.

Both Bill and Miata looked up. "Uh oh," Bill cackled, snatching one last piece of bread from Miata's fingers. Flying to the bars, the blue and gold bird landed, then hopped through onto Jacq's shoulder.

Sitting back, Miata took a slow, deep breath. "It weren't supposed to be endin' like this," he told her.

"With you behind bars?" Jacq questioned coldly. "I should think not."

Miata shook his head. "That not be what I be meanin'. I be meanin' this." He gestured between the two of them. "We was supposed to still be mates." Jacq remained silent.

"Tom were offerin' me a lot, an' he were sayin' there be no bloodshed." Miata got to his feet, and he slowly approached the twin. "But then he were wantin' ye an' the

gold. I told him he couldn't be havin' ye because he be undeservin'." Jacq's demeanor softened. Miata's eyes, blue as the sky, let him deep into her soul. "No matter how much either o' us be lovin' ye," he whispered, reaching out to touch her hair, which she had gotten in the habit of wearing down. "It were then that Tom were makin' plans o' his own. I ne'er told him aboot what we was suspectin' aboot the lockets."

Tears formed in Miata's eyes but refrained from sliding down his young cheek. "I ne'er meant to be betrayin' yer trust." Bill rubbed his nose on Jacq's shoulder. The thief put his finger on Jacq's lips and whispered, "I were unaware I be havin' a best friend, 'til I lost her."

Pulling away from him, Jacq walked back down the corridor, her head hanging and throbbing with the thudding of her heart. *He was in love with me all along? Why don't people just come out and say these things?* she thought to herself. Then she thought of Dante; she stopped dragging herself down the seemingly endless corridor. She wished so very much to understand all these things. Snatching the key off the wall, she hurried back to the young man's cell, and, slipping it into the cold lock, she swung the door wide open.

Miata, who'd sunk into a ball on the floor, sprang wildly to his feet at the sound of the door. He found himself staring at a young woman he thought he knew. Yet, here she went surprising him again. He took her image in: golden-brown hair draped about her shoulders, coins accentuating her apparel, and boots that reached her knees—all somehow accentuating her pretty figure and spunky character. The locket, half the reason for this expedition, hung about her neck. Her eyes were red, her brow contorted in uncertainty, her neck strained so that all her tendons protruded, and her breathing was awkward. Yet, there she stood, waiting to find the friend she had lost. *I be havin' no idea what to be sayin' to her*, he thought, taking a deep breath, wanting to say the perfect thing.

Jacq kept her gaze on Miata, willing him to speak. *Does he have nothing to say? I came back, and he has nothing to say? I don't know what to say.*

Miata uneasily rubbed the back of his neck and took a slow step forward. *I be all but barin' me soul to her and she be havin' nothin' to say to me?*

Jacq narrowed her eyes. *Why does he have nothing to say? Speak!* Taking a step toward him, Jacq opened her mouth. After several seconds, she found that she was able to mutter in a quiet voice that only one who was listening for it in earnest would be able to hear, "Miata..."

Smiling and blinking back tears, the young man took a few long strides forward, scooping her up into a warm embrace. Squawking irritably, Bill flew to the bars. Gasping and returning the gesture, she found she could squeak out not another word.

"Jacq." He sighed, setting her daintily back on her feet and cupping her face in his hands. "I be most sorry. I were ne'er wantin' this to be happenin'."

Swallowing her tears, Jacq shook her head. "Think naught of it." Pausing, she touched his cheek and looked him in the eye, allowing herself to smile. "Mate."

A wide smile stretching across his face, the thief leaned forward and kissed Jacq on the forehead, sighing heavily out threw his nose, not really realizing how incredibly

stressed he was until that point when he relaxed. Throwing his arms around her again, he chuckled. "I be guessin' yer sister shan't be happy aboot this."

At that, Jacq whispered, "Speaking of my sister, was there anything that Margaret left out in her story to Alex and Amy?" Searching his eyes keenly, Jacq's narrowed as she peeked at the sleeping woman in the cell next to them.

Looking to the ceiling for an answer, Miata admitted, "I be not one to be askin'. I ne'er heard a word aboot anything o' the sorts afore she tol' yer sisters." He grinned sheepishly. Jacq shook her head, a smirk of amusement lifting the corner of her mouth. Hastily, he added, "She were talkin' in her sleep though, an' perfect English it were."

Grabbing his wrist, Jacq pulled him along behind her. "Follow me. I have something to show you." The two hurried out his cell door, up the stairs, and out onto the top deck, Bill flying madly behind them.

Wincing in the bright sunshine he had not seen for weeks, Miata stumbled along behind Jacq toward the ship's edge. They stopped abruptly at the railing of the ship; he followed her finger across the waters to … land. Blinking several times, Miata then gaped at Jacq, who simply smiled and sighed. "I never thought I would wish to return to this place."

Across the ship, Alex saw the two, and her eyes grew twice their normal size. Tapping Mr. Bibbs, who was standing about arms' length away, she continued to gawk as the butler turned and joined her in the jaw-dropped ogle. "Is that what you meant by amend? Can she release him?" Alex murmured.

"Well, I don't know, Miss Alexandria…Nobody stopped her." Mr. Bibbs sighed. Glancing down at Alex, he inquired, "Have you made all your amends?"

Alex's mouth twisted downward. "Amends with *him*?" Alex folded her arms. "I would rather not like to."

"Of course, Miss Alexandria," Mr. Bibbs agreed. "It is not as if he'll be around…"

Rolling her eyes, Alex huffed at this and stalked off toward her twin.

"You're a shrewd man, Mr. Bibbs," Captain Turner's voice interrupted him. "Is there anything you do not have up your sleeve?"

Mr. Bibbs rotated to face the captain, and the two gentlemen stood face to face in similar tailored coats, their coattails hanging to their knees, their tri-corner hats just so on their perfectly done hair. "Caring for such a one," Mr. Bibbs eyed the twins over his shoulder, "is patience and leaves one with a feeling of achievement. Caring for such a one," his gaze returned to Viking Pierce, standing at the stern of the boat with a telescope, "is a hazard to one's health and a test of one's very survival skills."

The captain smiled. "Well said, Mr. Bibbs." Then, tipping his hat, Turner continued on his way. "Very well said, indeed."

Reaching Jacq's side, Alex grabbed her twin's uninjured arm. "Excuse us a moment," she said to Miata more out of habit than real apology. Once they were a small distance away, Alex growled, "Just what do you think you are doing, Jacq?"

"He did not really betray us," Jacq said to Alex, who was now standing akimbo in front of her twin. "I mean, he

kept our idea about the lockets a secret … And he actually tried to protect me from Tom …"

Folding her arms, Alex frowned irritably at this. "But what about his life? Is he going to stop stealing for good?"

"Why, Alex," Jacq said, "I didn't know you cared …!" Her lips parted in a teasing grin.

Glowering at her, Alex cleared her throat and crossed her arms. "If he intends to stay your friend, then of course I care …" Jacq grinned playfully at her. "Oh, come on!"

"He says he's changed his colors," Jacq said, matching her sister's stance.

Heaving a heavy sigh, Alex replied, "Very well."

Turning, the two were surprised to see Amy beaming up at their topic of discussion. He was smiling down softly at her, tracing her jaw with his fingers. Grabbing Jacq by the front of her shirt, Alex whispered between her teeth, "What in the name of England is *that*?" Jacq shrugged. "*Ugh!*"

The two twirled around just in time to see Amy stand on tiptoe for a kiss. Miata bent to satisfy her, but Alex yelped, "*Wait!*" Rushing forward and pulling Amy hurriedly away from his arms and grabbing her by the shoulders, Alex questioned, "What happened? What's going on?"

Still looking drunkenly at Miata, Amy replied, "He stole my heart…" Placing her hand daintily over her heart, she smiled faintly, continuing to look at him over her shoulder.

All eyes nearby turned to look at the curly-haired blond. Alex's nostrils flared. "That's nonsense!" Blazing, her gaze swept to Miata.

"It were unintentional, I be swearin' to that!" he spoke, cowering at the raging inferno before him.

Mr. Bibbs, who had sauntered over to the side of the deck they were on, eyed them a moment before clearing his throat and saying, "Hmm...Well, he *wasn't* part of the family..."

Touching Alex's shoulder, Jacq gave it a tight squeeze. "Let it go."

Turning heatedly to Jacq, Alex growled in raw frustration. "What is it with you? Both of you! Both of my sisters falling for thieves!"

"*Ex*-thieves," Jacq corrected nonchalantly, smiling at the wordplay. "Or *ex*-miscreants. That sounds even better."

Alex's eyes narrowed into slits of severe discontent. *If only I had a sword, I would protect Amy with my sword, my hatchet, my...*

Noticing that her sister was evolving into a warrior rather quickly, Jacq said, "Miata has pledged he shall never commandeer again."

Looking her twin dead in the eye, Alex leaned into her sister's face and asked in a hiss, "And you believe him?"

Miata's skin crawled at Alex's voice.

Returning the look with equal ferocity, Jacq, slanted forward, saying, "Aye."

A strange feeling came over him when he heard Jacq say that word. *Always me truest mate*, he thought soberly, forgetting the reason for their argument momentarily.

"How can you trust him?" Alex asked, looking Jacq up and down in disbelief.

"Sometimes you just have to trust yourself to believe," Jacq replied. She straightened her back, holding Alex's gaze evenly, reassuring herself that she believed her own words.

Alex's mental and emotional arsenal came clattering to the ground around her. Shifting her weight and keeping an even watch on Jacq, she internally took off her heavily plumed war helmet, setting it on the ground at her sister's feet. Nodding while she straightened out her yellow dress, she sighed. "Very well." Releasing Amy, the two watched her glide to Miata, who smiled at both of them. "Let us prepare to go ashore," Alex said, threading her arm between Jacq's arm and waist.

Jacq smirked as Alex tugged her down to their room, now shared with Amy as well. "It shall be nice to return to Port de Couler de Bateaux," she said. Watching her sister closely, Jacq sat quietly in her hammock.

Grabbing handfuls, Alex began shoving her small assortment of things into the bag she had received from the Bumbleridges. She looked over the cloak, the flintlock pistol, the compass, smiling faintly at the items in memory of the givers. Then, quite suddenly, she paused her hurried packing and asked, "What shall we do when we get there? We have no family, and we have no friends that are expecting our return." Her eyes glazing over, she spun to stare at Jacq for some sort of an answer.

Mulling the thoughts over silently, Jacq swayed back and forth in the hammock, holding her sister's gaze. Intertwining her fingers, she idly picked at her thumbnail while grimacing at Alex's yellow dress. "Well, first off, we find our treasure. With the proper clues now, we should have a better go at it...Then, once that business is finished with, perhaps we should go find our father." As she spoke her suggestion, she arched her eyebrow, awaiting her twin's reaction.

"Are you serious!" called Alex. "I mean, last Amy knew he was still alive, but he has thought we were dead all these years ... How do you know he would even want to see us?"

"I just know!" Folding her arms in front of her in disgust at such a question, Jacq sent Alex a frosty glare. "And I hope."

The two looked at each other, speaking nothing, but saying everything. "Perhaps the time is coming that we move on with our lives, discover what we are to do in life," Alex said. She turned away.

Jacq swallowed hard, wincing at the pain. "You mean go separate ways?"

"Jim has talked of marriage," Alex said, her thoughts drifting for a moment to the tall, dusty-haired man. "He has to go finish things he started before we met, but after that ..." She paused, returning her look to stare deep into Jacq's wet eyes.

Nodding, Jacq broke the locked stare, casting her gaze to the floor. "So, what do you wish to do while you wait for him?" A hushed calm filled the room while Jacq hung her head and Alex observed her, searching for a response. Feeling a slender, gloved hand touch her face, Jacq lifted her eyes to the face of the girl in the yellow dress.

"Perhaps maybe it would be best to go meet our father."

"But you said ..."

"I know what I said." Kneeling in front of Jacq, Alex recaptured her stare. "But I also know what you said." Involuntarily, Jacq's brow furrowed. Smiling, Alex continued,

"I do not know what tomorrow holds for us, sister, but someone told me that sometimes you just have to trust yourself to believe." She searched Jacq's face hopefully. "And I want to have that hope and faith as well."

Jacq's forehead smoothed, but her eyebrow arched. "But you just said…"

"I know." Alex laughed. "But, think about it. If Jim is going to be gone for a while, then what else have I to do? Besides, our father is worth our time. We have made it this far. What sort of person would I be to not pursue this with you? If I do not, I will regret it forever."

Shaking her head, Jacq couldn't keep the smile off of her face. "And what of Amy?"

"No doubt she will come with us," Alex said. "After all, he is her father too…And…I guess we could bring Miata with." Sighing, she returned to packing her bag. "I do not wish him to lose anyone else if it can be helped."

Scooping her things into her bag, Jacq yawned and stretched. "I agree. I shall be on deck."

She scurried to the dragon at the front of the ship. Gazing out toward Port de Couler de Bateaux, Jacq could hear Captain Taylor's voice in her ear. *Jacq, you are a special girl. You're the only one that I can travel the world with.* She saw the petals from Dante's bag falling onto the frothy sea below. She felt Captain Taylor's strong arms around her and his deep laugh booming about her, filling the air. "I didn't get to see the zebras," she whispered.

"Don't give up so easily, lass," a familiar voice said.

Twisting about, Jacq found herself staring up at Dante, his hair jet black against the fair blue sky. "But it's the truth. I didn't get to see them. I didn't even get near Africa."

Averting her eyes to the sea, she took a long, deep breath before saying, "And it looks like maybe I ne'er shall."

"Jacq." Dante sighed. She moved her gaze back to his face. "Jacq, I owe the good Captain Turner another year of service. Being a man of my word, I intend to fulfill that accord."

She nodded.

"When my time is up, I shall receive a vessel of my own." Reaching across the small distance that separated them, he set his hand on her shoulder. "Once you have finished searching for your family, I would like very much, if you haven't already been, to be"—Jacq held her breath—"the one who takes you to see the zebras."

Hesitating a moment, thinking perhaps she had not heard him correctly, Jacq asked, "Really? You mean that?" Rubbing the back of his neck, he smiled and nodded. Gasping, Jacq held herself back from flinging her arms about his neck and was hardly able to breathe properly. Jittering with excitement, she focused her energy on keeping her feet planted and maintaining a cool façade. "Thank you," she finally whispered breathlessly.

Cupping her cheek with his hand, Dante pushed all her hair out of her face and watched her for a few brief seconds. "I just hope it will make up for our misunderstandings."

Taking his hand in her own, Jacq whispered, "It means much more than that, mate." Pausing, she admired his helter-skelter hairdo and smiled. "Much, much more."

Chapter 11

A cold autumn had set Port de Couler de Bateaux to sleep while the twins were away. A still layer of fog had settled down amongst the townsfolk as though it was one of them. Almost all of the vegetation had crawled back underground or retired its painters for the season. There was a cool stillness about the whole of the port that muffled all the sound and movement throughout. An apprehensive chill sat on its haunches, watching the ship approach. Somewhere within the town, a bell tolled, echoing off of the low-hanging clouds and snug buildings. Everywhere, oil lamps flickered in windows as if welcoming the voyagers back home.

Nudging Alex, Jacq pointed at the two docile vessels that sat docked in the harbor waters. "It looked much like this the first day I arrived," she whispered, "eight and a half years ago."

The quiet of the port crept across the sea and engulfed the *Sea Dragon* and her crew. It hushed their mouths and their thoughts, drawing them to the railing to admire its small city. Swirling coolly about them, it insisted the girls put their cloaks on and reminded them it was prepping for winter now. They had missed most of the warm summer months; autumn was short.

Captain Turner turned to address his men. "We can stay but one or two nights, lads. We must gather our necessary supplies afore we follow these," he waved his arm at the girls, Miata, Pierce, Bibbs, Dante, and Jim, "to where the buried treasure may be." At this, groans drifted up around the ship. "Belay your moanin'!" he ordered. "We shall set sail the day after the morrow. Any questions?" Of course, there were none—only snide remarks the sailors kept quiet.

Once the *Sea Dragon* was docked in the harbor, the girls raced down the ramp along with the boatswain, Miata, the first mate, and Viking Pierce. Jacq led the way; the others followed her in pairs: Alex and Jim, Miata and Amy, Dante and Pierce. The group hurried to the burned down inn, which was exactly as it had been when they left, per request of the girls to have all left untouched until their return. The cool, wintery weather bit at them as they scurried to where the door of the inn used to stand.

Pulling out a piece of parchment from her sash, Jacq read, "*At the inn, turn your back, to the SW sea / Across the way lies the key / True to the marker stay and it will lead ye / At last to dig in sand to set the treasure free.*" Glancing behind them, the sea shimmered like glass, reflecting the cold sky above. Pulling out her compass, Jacq verified the southwest direction. Rotating to *across the way*, they saw the blacksmith's shop. The group stood, staring, for several seconds. "The blacksmith?" Jacq muttered aloud,

speaking for all standing there. She noticed, however, a distinctive sword shape on display as part of his sign. *The marker,* she reasoned inwardly.

Taking a deep breath, she tucked the compass back into her pocket, grabbed Alex by the wrist, and towed her gaping sister across the street. They were not surprised to find the blacksmith hammering away at a shovel. "Good day, Henry," Jacq called out to him.

The burly, bearded man set down his things and turned a broad grin to the girls. "Ah!" he said cordially. "There ye be! I been waitin' fer ye to arrive." His thick, rolling accent curled about them like the charcoal gray smoke from his hot furnace as he spoke.

"You have?" the two girls asked in unison, dumbfounded expressions blanketing their faces.

"Aye." He laughed, limping into the back of his shop. "Yer guardians, rest their souls, had me make these gifts afore they passed away," he called as he rummaged through some things in the back. Within a few moments, Henry reappeared from the recesses of his shop, carrying two shovels. "This one be fer ye, an' this one fer ye." Proudly giving one to each girl, he smiled broadly, crossing his soot smudged arms in satisfaction of a job well done. "Beauties, aren't they?"

"Aye," Jacq said awkwardly, turning the tool upside down so that the handle was pointing to the ground and the actual shovel was level with her eyes.

Henry nodded, grinning as if he'd just accomplished the most important task in the world. "Yer guardians, rest their souls, paid me good fer these here shovels. An' they paid me t'keep 'em 'til ye came a lookin' fer 'em," he added excitedly.

Rather stunned and holding out the shovel like a foreign object she'd never seen before, Alex frowned, saying, "I am afraid I do not understand."

Grabbing a hold of Alex's wrist again, Jacq laughed. "Thank you, Henry! If e'er we need a blacksmith, you shall be the one we come to!" With that, the girl took off, dragging her sister along behind her.

"Haha!" Henry's voice boomed. "Yer good lasses! Always were!"

"What are you doing?" Alex asked, yanking her arm free of Jacq's grasp once they had reached the inn again.

Breathlessly, Jacq snatched her twin's shovel from her hands, turned it upside down, and gave it back to her. "What do you see?" she asked, her breath barely beginning to regulate. The others gathered around the girl in the yellow dress.

Her eyes growing at this, Alex let out a long, slow breath. "More riddles."

"Oh no!" Jacq grinned eagerly. "This is the rest of the riddle. Just as my locket had to be read first, so does my shovel. But they make no sense alone. To make sense, they have to be together, with yours." Her eyes glinted and she hugged her shovel, a wave of intense enthusiasm overtaking her.

Dante could do nothing but grin and watch the wide-eyed girl dance about giddily with her new tool.

Alex sighed. "You are enjoying this entirely too much."

Taking her twin's shovel again, Jacq held them side by side and read, "*Under the boards ye must go. To the left of the hearth.*"

Twirling about as one, the cluster stared at the scattered ashes, now mostly dirt and charred stubs of wood. Picking her way to where the fireplace made of brick once blazed proudly for all company at Midway Zebra, Jacq stared down at the black floor. Lifting her shovel, she thrust it down on the boards to the left of the brick. Splintering agreeably at the force of the tool, the charred pieces scattered about her feet. Everyone leaned in to try and get a better look. Prying up the boards, Jacq suddenly stopped and turned a worried look to Alex.

Gathering her clean skirts, Alex hurried to the other girl and whispered, "What is wrong?"

"There is no sand beneath these boards," Jacq said, her face contorting as she rethought her theory. Glancing to the blacksmith's shop then casting her gaze to the ocean, she mentally retraced her steps, inaudibly reciting the clues.

Dropping her skirts, Alex's eyes suddenly glowed. "In the kitchen! The hearth in the kitchen!"

Jacq blinked. Taking a step toward her twin, she leaned to her ear and in a low tone asked, "There was a hearth in the kitchen?"

Rolling her eyes, Alex cleared her throat and glared good-naturedly at her twin. "Perhaps if you had washed the dishes once in a while, you would have known."

Her mouth curving half in amusement and half in mocking, Jacq looked at the sky and then squinted at Alex. "Are you trying to make me feel guilty for not washing the dishes? Because if you are, it's not working."

Smiling at her sister's play, Alex grabbed her wrist and escorted her to where the kitchen once stood.

"What's going on?" Viking Pierce asked, straining to see between the others.

"They be searchin' still," Miata said.

Listening to Pierce and Miata, Dante's face lit up with a bit of a smirk. Then, looking back to the girls, he noticed them fidgeting with the tools. His mouth picking up at the corner, he heaved a sigh and marched out to them. The rest of the group took a step forward, wondering what hint of gold the boatswain had seen to draw him out.

Jacq and Alex were shifting their hands uncomfortably on the shovel handles when Dante reached them. Holding out his hand and glancing at the sand they'd uncovered, he offered, "May I?"

The two girls glanced at the others only to see Jim begin walking towards them, holding out his hand as well. Shrugging, Jacq handed her tool to Dante as Alex gave hers to Jim. Stepping back in unison, the twins kept their eyes on the hole they had started. Shoving the metal down into the sand, Jim pulled out a quarter of the total amount of sand the girls had accumulated altogether after much effort on their part in one haul. Dante followed suit, winking at Jacq when he emptied his load onto the pile.

Back and forth the two young men went, becoming shiny with sweat, their muscles rippling for all to see in the cool air. The girls watched in dismay as their pit increased one foot...two feet...Others from the ship began to appear now, filing in after fulfilling the orders given them by Captain Turner.

By the end of half an hour of digging in the cold, damp sand, Captain Turner and Mr. Bibbs arrived, Frank and Bill with them, eager to rejoin their owners. Seeing Jacq standing not too far off, Bill took flight. As he settled himself down on her shoulder, his eye caught sight of the hole, and, staring down at its growing mouth, he squawked, "Uh oh!"

A dull *tink* resounded from the end of Dante's shovel. Everyone exchanged glances, the air falling completely silent for a few breath-held moments. Then, as if started by a gun, the two girls flung themselves into the hole, unearthing with their hands what had been searched for with shovels. Bill flew to Mr. Bibb's white head of hair and began to screech angrily at the commotion. Bending their backs to pull the strongbox from the hands of the sands, they could barely breathe as everyone surrounding them helped pull it from its grave.

Tracing the edging, made of the same material as their lockets, Jacq radiated with pride while Alex stared in disbelief. "I did not realize," Alex said quietly, "that I did not believe it was real."

"Never mind that." Jacq laughed excitedly, waving her hand to dismiss her skepticism. "We must now discover the secret of how to open it."

Kneeling beside her, Dante pointed to a heart-shaped outline in the metal edging. She stared at him, admitting with her gaze she did not understand. Gesturing at the locket around her neck, Dante whispered, "They shall not find a heart in this man. He either gave it away, or buried it with his treasure. Which do you think?"

"He gave it to a little girl," she whispered, pulling the locket from her shirt. Holding her hand out to Alex, she insisted, "Give me your locket!"

Alex, stunned and soiled from head to toe, pulled her locket off and held it out to Jacq. How its golden luster shone in the drab autumn air! Seizing it from her, Jacq placed the two lockets side by side, hers on the left. The intricate patterns engraved on their closed surfaces were beyond compare. Placing the two halves in the heart outline, the piratical-looking twin, her coins jingling only from gusts of wind, held her breath and pushed on the lockets, which clicked into place. Gleefully, she reached her hand up slowly to the lid. Everyone pushed in closer, straining for even a peek. Giving a hardy push to the chest top, her heart stopped. It didn't budge!

Whirling about to Dante, she said between her teeth, "It didn't work!"

Gently touching her shoulder, he said in a hushed tone, "I know. I saw."

Jacq's mind raced. What was wrong? What had she forgotten? She had put the key in the lock... "Oh!" Jacq giggled, letting one hand fall onto Dante's shoulder. "We have to turn the key." As she spoke, she raised her right hand to the heart, placing a finger on each half, and pushing as hard as she could, rotated the piece to the right.

As another click sprang from the box, the crowd gasped and fell silent. Looking up at Alex, Jacq invited, "Shall we?"

Taking a knee beside her, Alex smiled through the soot and sand and dust that littered her dress and her face. "We

shall." She smiled, a rush of excitement coursing through her veins as her fingers touched the cool surface of the chest.

Placing their hands on the edge of the lid, the twins readied themselves and then together pushed the heavy strongbox open, displaying not only gold, but jewels the likes of which they had never seen before. Cheers sprang up from everyone; the entire crew had arrived by this time.

Her eyes wider than when a child gets its first toy on Christmas morning, Jacq spun to her sister and gasped, covering her mouth with her sandy, crusted fingers. "We did it! We found their treasure! Treasure they left for us!"

"And we got rid of our enemies!" They suddenly both stopped and saw in their minds a green-eyed, redheaded woman glowering at them from beneath carefully preened eyebrows. "Well," she stammered awkwardly, "most of our enemies."

"See," Jacq smiled, satisfied as she watched everyone dance joyfully about her, "you should just trust me."

"No, that would not work either." She sighed glumly, watching Amy and Miata hug and twirl about amongst the other crewmen who were laughing, slapping each other's backs, and eyeing the find eagerly.

"What?" Jacq retorted, turning a rather confused look toward her sister as she pushed hair back from her forehead, leaving dirty streaks. "Why would that not work?"

"Because," Alex said. A sad smile stretching her lips, she faced her twin. "You are most often right when I believe you to be wrong."

"Nay." Jacq laughed. "That is not so." *Except with Margaret, the treasure, the pirates, the lockets, Miata, Dante, Viking Pierce...* Shuddering, she shook her head, smiled somewhat painfully, and acknowledged, "Aye, perhaps you are right."

"So…" Alex smiled, dusting off part of her dress but leaving handprints where she touched it. "How do we divide this up between, what, fifty people?" Glancing about her at all the heads moving up and down and side to side, she soon gave up the idea of counting.

"Fifty-eight, to be exact," Mr. Bibbs reported primly from behind them.

Springing to her feet, Jacq flung her arms about his waist and suddenly felt ever so small. Glancing about awkwardly, the butler then gave in and returned the embrace. Opening her eyes, she saw Captain Turner standing behind the butler, his hands clasped behind his back as always. When his stern but kind face smiled down at her, she thought she could see not one man—not two men—but three. Lessening her grip on Mr. Bibbs, she straightened and approached the captain. Letting her go, the butler then twisted to smile at Alex. However, as he rotated back to look at her, she gave him a sheepish smile and snuggled into his arms as well. His eyes watering, he pulled her close as well, smoothing her hair.

As Jacq stared at the grand man before her, decorated and dressed in his dark blue coat outlined with white and yellow accents, her mind wondered, *Is this Captain Turner, Captain Taylor, or my father?*

Winking, the man took a step forward and said, "You're going to be just fine, Miss Jacqueline."

Without hesitation, Jacq rushed into his arms, and, squeezing him tightly, she thought, *Perhaps he is all of them.* A calm feeling came over her, and she closed her eyes.

175

Stunned by her response, the captain patted her lightly on the back a few seconds before caving in and returning her excessively exuberant embrace.

"Thank you for everything, Captain Turner," she whispered, realizing that she was trying not to cry. "You have done much for me in allowing me passage on your ship."

"Captain Taylor and your father would be proud," his deep voice told her in a low tone.

Pulling away, Jacq stared up at him. "Did you know my father?" The dark fog that had surrounded them began quite suddenly to dissipate, and a brilliant sun peeked through the heavy mist, sending a ray down to shine on them.

Taking her chin in his hand, he brushed away the strands of hair from her face and whispered, "Nay, lass. I *know* your father."

"Then," Jacq paused breathlessly, "he's alive?" Smiling, Captain Turner nodded. "Did you know Amy and Margaret then? Why didn't you speak of this before now?"

"I had never before seen Miss Amy, but Miss Margaret, I knew. She did not recognize me, however; I thought it best to wait," he said, putting his arm about her shoulders.

"But, you could not have known Alex and I were his daughters." She searched his face for an answer. "Or did you?"

"You both look a lot like your mother, may she now rest in peace. I attended their wedding, and I never forget a face, especially not one as sweet as hers."

"And you have seen my father since then?" Jacq's question got the attention of both Alex and Mr. Bibbs.

A crooked smile curving his lips, Captain Turner tapped her nose with his finger and whispered, "Aye, lass.

We sailed together since his other daughter, Miss Amy, was born. He is alive and quite well. And, I know, without question, that he would love to meet both you and Miss Alexandria..."

Continuing to leave her arm about his waist, Jacq twisted and smiled at Alex. Throwing herself forward, Alex buried her face in Jacq's shoulder. "We have found a sister and our father." She sniffled, holding both her twin and the captain in a group hug.

"Aye." Jacq sighed, glancing about her. "We have won many of the battles we have fought as of late." Her eyes coming to rest on Dante, she held in a sigh.

"I believe we have won them all," Alex said contentedly, fastening her vision on Jim, who was smiling kindly in her direction.

Shrugging and averting her gaze, Jacq forced a small smile onto her face. "Perhaps."

Chapter 12

Dropping her things on the floor beside the hotel room bed she had for the night, Jacq reached down and touched the blankets, fanning her fingers out over their soft, inviting surface. A strange smile—the kind one gets when remembering something they thought had been forgotten—stretched her lips. Then, taking a leap into the air, she let herself tumble onto the mattress, bouncing up in the air, all the bedding getting tossed into the air around her.

She giggled quietly to herself as the pillows and blankets settled about her. Stretching her entire body as long as she could, she took in a long, even breath and as she relaxed, she let it back out. "A real bed . . ." Grabbing one of the pillows, she looked at its smooth surface, tracing the edge with her fingertips as she continued talking aloud to herself hardly above a whisper. "Of course, the hammocks were nice too, really. All the talk about them being uncomfortable was absolute rubbish."

Hearing a few footsteps emitting near the foot of the bed, Jacq pushed herself up to a sitting position, setting the pillow down, and involuntarily took a sharp inhale of breath. Slapping her hand over her mouth, she stifled a laugh. At the end of her bed stood Alex, her lengthy, strawberry-blonde locks partially pulled up, allowing half of her hair to cascade down her back. Her attractively shaped figure was donning a new dress, which almost shimmered in the dimming evening and oil lamp light.

"Is it that bad?" she asked, smoothing the silky, pink skirts. "I was afraid it cost too much and is too plain."

Jacq looked over her twin's outfit, somehow managing to keep the corner of her mouth from bending upwards. The dress was a radiant pink with exquisite white laces sewn here and there about the hems and other accenting parts of the gown. She had also obtained white gloves that reached from her fingertips to her elbows. Looking as golden as the locket that hung around her exposed throat, locks of hair fell about her face from the fancy, upper-class arrangement atop her head. If there was some flaw in her dressing, Jacq was not going to find it. The girl simply glowed in the light, and she challenged the dazzle of the brightest star with the light that shone from her eyes and her smile.

"Aside from the fact that you are wearing a dress, you look…" Alex's eyes widened with concern; amused with herself, Jacq held the pause, continuing to assess her sister's apparel, then concluded, "perfect."

Relieved, Alex grinned and whispered giddily, "We are to dine for supper. A *proper* supper! Is that not so very exciting?" Her eyes sparkled, and she clapped her hands with excitement.

"Oh...How lovely..." Nodding, Jacq gave her sister a tight smile as she pulled her cloak out of her luggage on the floor then put it around her shoulders for warmth. Supper? What was *she* to do for supper? All of her friends were busy being friends with their other friends. She did not want to spend the evening with Amy and Miata; she did not wish to be a witness to anything. Everyone she'd want to spend dinner with already had made plans...

Noticing her quiet demeanor, Alex bit her lower lip and scooted closer. "Would...would you want to dine with us?" she asked, sitting daintily on the edge of the bed beside her.

Leaning back onto her elbows, Jacq smiled softly, her heart warming at the offer. "Nay, sister. I insist you enjoy your first proper supper with Jim by yourself..." Alex didn't look convinced. "Perhaps next time I'll join you."

"Are you certain?" the twin asked. She leaned forward and narrowed her eyes as she scrutinized Jacq's nonverbal communication.

"Of course!" Jacq insisted. She laughed and gave Alex's shoulder a gentle shove. "Now, if you're not already, go finish preparing for your evening."

A short while later, Jacq found herself waving Alex and Jim off, leaving her in the room by herself.

Quietly, she and Bill, who had been napping on a chair in the room, pulled out her things from the bag: the empty pistol, the gunpowder, the bullets, and the bags of jewels and treasure she had packed away. As she held the pistol in her hand, an odd feeling crawled over her. She could suddenly smell the smoke from it after it was shot. Her muscles recounted the feel of the recoil in her arm. An uneasy feeling pushed into her stomach as she recalled Tom crumpling to the ground. She stared at the cold metallic object as though it was gazing intently at her. The longer she looked at it, the more she thought she felt her breathing growing shallow and as though she could not rip her eyes from it. Finally, after several seconds, she dropped it back into the bag, kicking the bag under the bed.

Backing away from it, she felt her heart beat pounding in her neck and her breath uneasy, making her chest rise and fall rapidly. She sighed, trying to regulate her breathing, and scooped Bill tenderly into her arms as she used to do when she was very small. "Life changes, doesn't it, Bill?" Walking to the window, she could barely see where the Midway Zebra remains lay strewn about in their above-ground grave. Cooing, Bill closed his eyes and snuggled up to Jacq's chin. "It seems like it's stuck in a rut for so long and then, one day, you get up and the cart is nowhere to be seen. Hundreds of other carts fill the streets, and the entire world around you has changed."

Shadows danced about on the ground outside, allowing Jacq to watch in total secrecy as the dancers inside the inn below her laughed and twirled around. Occasionally, she could hear Dante telling the end of a tale and the immediate roar of approval from his listeners. As one of these uproars died down, there was a loud rap on her door. Frank, who'd been reclining in a chair, squabbled something fierce about it as he sprang to Alex's bed. Bill's eyes popped open, but he remained calm. Jacq spun about and swung the door wide open.

"The party favorite is up here alone? That just doesn't seem quite right," a deep voice said as a tall, clean-shaven man invited himself in and sat in Frank's chair.

"It sounded like you had that covered," Jacq said. Letting Bill up to her shoulder, she sat on the edge of her bed, folding her hands in her lap.

Shrugging and adjusting the collar of his new, crisp, white shirt, Dante said, "I can recall a good story and make a grand yarn. However, everyone wishes to see you." Eyeing her, he tried to read her mood. "Why don't you come down there with me? You shall see." A spunky smile blossomed onto his tanned face.

"Do they not wish to see Alex also? And what of Amy? They are my sisters. Will they not do?" Crossing her arms stubbornly over her stomach, she inclined an eager ear for his answer.

Standing and towering gloriously above her, Dante gestured with his head for her to follow. "Come on, Jacq." Standing up slowly, she eyed him. Putting his arm around her shoulders, he began gently escorting her out the door, saying, "Alex is with Jim. Amy already met everyone downstairs and then disappeared with the lad."

"Miata?"

"Aye." Jacq grimaced. Smiling, Dante continued, "The truth is, you are the only one of the three they have not seen tonight; the only one who is sitting alone in her room while everyone wishes to see her, and all because you do not have an invitation to join them."

Jacq's eyes suddenly glinted, and every inch of her shone. Rather astonished by this instantaneous transformation, Dante could not help but stare. "Then we shan't

keep the good people waiting!" she said gallantly. Jacq's pace, previously flatfooted and unwilling, quickened to match that of Dante's, and the two hurried to the lower level. Cheers rose sporadically around the room, yet all present raised their glasses and mugs, nodding in recognition of her entrance.

A crooked smirk formed on Dante's swarthy chiseled face. *Wouldn't you know it? She has no idea I just used them as an excuse to have her company, and look what happens. I mightn't get it anyway.*

Jacq sighed as she smiled and waved at the faces she knew amongst the numbers. *I wish Dante wished to have my company as these people do. But then, why would a lad with everything wish to have the company of one such as I?* The two smiled placidly at each other and walked to a table in the center of the hall. Several of the younger single men followed them. Who was this girl they had been near for eight years and not gotten to know? Who was this man she had brought back with her?

"So, tell me, Jacq," Dante ventured as they seated themselves across from one another, "how many of these lads are you mates with?"

Glancing casually about, Jacq wagged her head side to side as she counted and guestimated in her mind. "Seven of them. The others I have either hardly spoken to or never even seen before."

Dante could not help but stare at her and then cast a glance about the room himself. "Only seven? Out of all these?" He had counted at least forty different lads who had asked about her.

Nodding, Jacq smiled at someone. "Aye. There may be ten."

"Was he one of them?"

"I've never seen him afore in my life," she whispered, grinning with amusement.

Dante roared. Noticing that a crowd was beginning to gather and press themselves toward their little table, Dante cleared his throat. "Shall we play a game?"

Following his observant gaze, Jacq leaned forward and inquired in a low voice, "What kind of game?"

"Miss Luray?" one of the high society boys, who she'd previously seen but barely exchanged a greeting with, interrupted.

"Aye?" she acknowledged him, casting a glance at his scholarly face.

"Would you care to accompany me to the floor?" Moving his pasty, be-ruffled hand out in a weak gesture toward the smiling, dancing conglomeration of people twirling about, his lips strained into a smile.

Jacq could feel her insides cringing. She had to fight to keep her outsides from following suit. *It would be very appropriate of you to say yes*, part of her admitted. *But it wouldn't be nice because you won't say yes to anything else this chump asks you*, she countered. Smiling as politely as she could, Jacq replied, "No thank you, good sir. My mate and I are playing a game." Both she and the noodle-colored gentleman turned their eyes to Dante.

"Aye!" Dante said awkwardly, fishing for words, pulling cards from his pocket and beginning to shuffle them as he brought them atop the table. "Would you care to join?" He smiled convincingly.

"No thank you, good sir," he said, almost mocking Jacq. "There are many young lasses on this floor tonight who would love to dance."

Pathetic, Dante thought to himself, his smile becoming smug. "Very well."

Eww! Jacq's mind screamed. Forcing an awkward, self-conscious grin, Jacq shrugged, saying, "Perhaps another time."

Bowing, the man pivoted without another word and marched himself over to a gaggle of girls, giggling about all the well-dressed men they saw on the floor.

Turning back to Dante, Jacq stuck her nose in the air, a thin-lipped smile on her face, the very likeness of the snooty inquirer. Dante gave a shout of laughter, drawing unwanted attention. Taking notice of this, they hunkered down closer to the table, and Jacq shot him an impish grin. "So what's the game?"

He smiled. "Go fish."

For the next hour, the two played cards. Viking Pierce was perched on a chair nearby, occasionally dancing with a girl that happened his way or stopping by their table to exchange a few words, though he seemed quite distracted. He had traded in his rugged clothes for more civilized attire, wearing a pair of expensive trousers and boots topped off with a stylish shirt. At another table across the room from them, Captain Turner and Mr. Bibbs sat puffing on pipes and sharing a bottle of ale. "What," Mr. Bibbs's stuffy voice spoke, slow and even, "do you suppose shall come of them?"

Taking a long, thoughtful drag on his pipe, Captain Turner replied, "I have no idea, Mr. Bibbs. However,

I think, in their case, they are better off that way." He watched Dante laugh at Jacq, who smiled smugly and then snatched away the card he held out towards her.

"I meant the girls, Captain."

"Of course!" Turner agreed, recovering quickly from the realization of his misinterpretation. "However, I think that answer goes for either scenario. For you see, if the girls knew of their father's whereabouts and health, the likelihood of them embarking to search for him in the same manner they plan to now is almost nonexistent." In acknowledgement of his point, Mr. Bibbs nodded. "There is a difference between knowing the morrow and living the morrow. Those who know the morrow always worry it is happening the way it is predicted. Those who live the morrow are too busy living it the way it is supposed to happen to care it is as would be predicted."

"Wise words, Captain. Perhaps they shall be written in a book some day."

Turner grinned, his skin wrinkling at the corners of his eyes. "If my words are to be written, then may it also say an old mate said them to me once as well."

"Then may it be so," Mr. Bibbs said. Pulling the pipe from his mouth, he watched the smoke rise from the smoldering end of his pipe. "May it be so."

Out of the corner of his eye, Dante noticed the two men watching Jacq and him play their card game. "Ahoy," he whispered. "It appears we have an audience across the way."

"What?" Jacq glanced over her shoulder and caught a glimpse of the captain and the butler between the twirling dancers.

"Aye," Dante said, "they're keepin' a sharp eye on us." Sitting back in his chair, he laughed.

"Perhaps we should get some fresh air and see if they have a mind to follow us," she suggested. A sly expression formed her facial features as she flopped her cards on the table and pushed them to the center.

Dante grinned, pulling the cards to himself and beginning to shuffle them. "Fresh air, eh? Very well…" He glanced around the room. "Let us exit through that door over there." Following his gaze to one not too far away, Jacq smiled. "My cloak's just there, and maybe we can catch a glimpse of that moonlit sea."

All but springing out of their seats, the two scurried to the door and clambered out virtually unnoticed, Dante snatching up his cloak on the way. As they rounded the corner of the inn, Jacq stopped dead in her tracks. Running into her, Dante said, "Hey! What…"

Slapping her hand over his mouth, Jacq held her finger up in front of her lips and gestured to a pair of figures by the seashore. "Don't disturb the stargazers. It's very impolite, you know," she told him in a hushed tone.

"What?" Dante asked when she removed her hand. "How can you tell if they're lookin' at stars or not? In fact, they are so close together, how can you even tell there are two people over there?" Squinting at the figures, he was unaware of Jacq's eyebrow-raised glare.

"Should I get you a telescope?" she asked sarcastically, shoving her fists onto her hips.

"No, no," he said, not recognizing her facetious tone as he continued looking at the couple. "Say, I think you're right."

Rolling her eyes, Jacq slapped her hand onto her forehead.

"And it looks to be Miss Amy!"

First throwing her arms in the air, then grabbing him by the wrist and dragging him back around the corner, Jacq said, "Silence yourself! You could wake the dead."

"Did you not wish to know it was your sister and Miata?" Dante returned, glancing down at her hand clenching his wrist to avoid her sharp, boring stare.

"Nay!" Jacq exclaimed in an impressively low tone of voice. "For if one was to tell me such a thing and then another to ask me about it later, I could not honestly say I knew not of what the second was saying...Savvy?" Releasing her hold on his wrist and folding her arms, she eyed him intently, wishing he could have figured it all out on his own and that she could be mad at him.

"Oh." He smiled in sudden understanding. "You wish to be free of responsibility."

"Aye." She rubbed the side of her head.

"So you wish to be irresponsible?" he asked.

"I said no such thing!" Her eyes narrowed at him for putting words in her mouth.

"But you do not wish to be responsible," Dante said.

"You are attempting to make me feel guilty about knowing what's going on." Her foot began to tap on the cobblestone street.

"That's preposterous! Why would I do that?" Dante asked, reeling back at her accusation.

"I'm not quite sure, but it's working," she said, glaring at him with every feature in her face and every muscle in her body.

"So what are you going to do about it?" he asked, crossing his arms in a way to imitate her.

Saying nothing, Jacq rolled her eyes and turned away, drumming her fingers where they rested on her arms. She had been an older sister for Alex on and off, but this was awful! Plus, Dante wasn't helping matters much with the reverse psychology ploy.

"You could just walk right up to them and interrupt," he said, his voice tempered with humor, "or…"

Jacq's face suddenly brightened and her back straightened. A devilish smile pinned the corners of her lips up. "I've an idea!"

I couldn't tell. Dante sighed. *Never would have guessed.*

Grabbing him again by the wrist, she whispered, "Come, come." Leading him around to the opposite corner, she noticed who she presumed to be Jim and Alex—she thought she could barely make out Alex's hair in the low lighting—sighing beneath the moonlight much further down the beach. Pulling her cloak tightly around her shoulders and up onto her head, she stepped casually out onto the sandy yard the inn kept. However, as she put her foot forward, she realized she was alone. Spinning about, she beckoned to Dante to join her. "Come, come! This is your idea. You must walk with me."

Dante sighed, lugging himself out to her side as he pulled his hood on as well. "I must learn when to keep my mouth shut."

"I agree," Jacq said, walking lightly toward Amy and Miata. Dante smiled down at her as she stared ahead, completely unaware of his smirking glance. "What do you think I should say to her?" Jacq whispered suddenly.

Dante jumped internally, startled at the breaking of the silence. "Uh … Tell her … Tell her … Uh, I don't know, Jacq. I could tell you how to tell a sailor he needs to do a better job with his swabbing, but sisterly advice is not really my area of expertise," he said. He smiled awkwardly though she was not looking at him, feeling useless on the topic.

"Don't feel bad. It's really not too much of a surprise," she replied.

"Well, I mean, if she was some pretty, plucky lass who wouldn't do what she was told, then I might have some advice," he returned, glaring at her slightly. However, at his retort, he clamped his mouth, stunned at his direct and flippant comment.

"What?"

His mouth wrinkled in disappointment at his carelessness. Holding his breath, he began to dream up things to say when she responded with …

"What does that have to do with it?" Jacq laughed. Dante relaxed, softly releasing his breath. "But thank you," Jacq added after a pause, smiling to herself. *How do you like that?*

Dante thought his heart stopped in his throat. His eyes shot down to stare at the top of her hooded head. "Sure," he heard his voice return in a deep, soft tone. *How do you like that?*

Unable to keep the crooked smile off of her face, Jacq cast Dante a blushing glance and then hastened her step.

Dante grinned, easily catching up to her with his long-legged gait.

In a few more strides, Jacq came up behind Amy. "Good evening," she said, glancing at Miata, who blushed.

190

"Hello, sister." Amy giggled, her eyes bursting with passion and breathless joy. "I pray your evening finds you well."

"It does," Jacq said, "but yours does not." Amy's eyes widened, and Jacq hid her amusement well enough not even Miata could see it. "Our sister is just yonder, so I will ask of you only two things." She held up the index and middle finger of her left hand. Amy nodded. "One," she held up only her index finger, "giggle loudly." Dante stared down at the top of her hood again; Amy smiled. "And two," she added back in her middle finger to hold up a total of two once again, "whether you have already done so or not, do not give this lad another kiss this night."

Flushing slightly, Amy agreed. "Yes, sister. I shall do as you ask." Giggling in her little high-pitched tone, Amy winked.

"Good lass," Jacq whispered; then she turned, hitting Miata in the shoulder as she did so. "You should know better!"

He swallowed an embarrassed lump in his throat and forced a weak smile onto his face. "I be takin' care not to be crossin' any lines ye be wantin' to be pummelin' me for." His eyes and voice were filled with assurance on the matter.

Sending him a warning glare, she nodded. "I should hope so ..." Then, turning, she trotted back toward the inn.

Shaking his head, Dante trotted after her. However, halfway there, he reached forward abruptly, stopping them both as he grasped her shoulder. Raising her eyes, Jacq swore his black hair bled right into the night sky. His dark eyes reflected the stars, though he was not looking at them. "We almost forgot!" he exclaimed.

Jacq gulped and her heart skipped a beat at his warm touch, staring into his dark, dark midnight-colored eyes. "Forgot what?"

"The sea," he reminded, turning her so she was facing it, "at night." Glancing down as her hood, loosened by him spinning her about, slipped off and fell to her shoulders, exposing her bare head, he smiled. She had left her bandana in her room when he so hastily escorted her out the door earlier. Pieces of her loose hair floated gently in the little gusts of wind that floated in from the ocean. "Isn't it beautiful?"

"Aye." Jacq sighed dreamily, watching the dark water roll forward and leave in a frothy hurry. "It is beautiful."

Amy giggled.

Standing at the window in the inn, Captain Turner stared out a few moments, then returned to his seat across from Mr. Bibbs. "Aye, Mr. Bibbs. They're goin' to be just fine."

"And, tell me, my good man, what are we to do with Miss Margaret?" Mr. Bibbs inquired bluntly, puffing on his pipe.

Blowing a smoke ring, Captain Turner sighed. "We shall have to allow Miss Amy to decide what she wishes to be done when we leave on the morrow. She is being held by the port keeper for the moment."

Later that night, after Jacq was nestled under her covers and beginning to drift off to sleep, she was jarred awake at hearing a key in the lock and then the door creak slowly open. Cracking her eye open, she peeked over the edge of the blankets to see a finely dressed young lady slip inside the room and press the door closed again as

carefully and quietly as she could with her gloved hands. "What're you doing?" Jacq asked a bit above a whisper as the other girl started to sneak across the floor.

"Ah!" Alex whirled about, touching her hand to heart. "I did not know you would still be awake. You gave me a shock!"

Hiding her smile behind her covers, Jacq returned, "So sorry…"

Her mouth turning into a half smile, Alex crossed back over and sat next to her on the bed. "You are not…"

Jacq giggled.

Jabbing her twin, Alex laughed. "Scoot over!" Jacq obliged. "Did your evening go well?" She stretched out on the bed next to her.

"Well enough," Jacq said, handing her a pillow to lean against. "And yours?"

"It was grand." Even in the light, Jacq could see Alex's eyes twinkling in supreme satisfaction as she snuggled with the cushion. "What about Amy?" she asked in a low tone.

"She's here in bed," Jacq assured her. She saw Alex was burbling with excitement beneath her skin. "What's going on? You seem awfully giddy…"

"Me?" Alex asked, sounding shocked Jacq would say such a thing.

"You're joking, right?" Jacq laughed, shaking her head and leaning forward to get a closer look at her smile-creased face.

Cuddling more with her pillow, she let out a light-hearted sigh. "*Well*, after we had our supper, we went for a little stroll on the beach outside of the inn…"

"Uh huh …" Jacq eyed her sister as best as she could in the dark room.

"It was lovely … Just lovely … We watched the sea roll in and draw back out. It was wonderful …" She paused, recounting the evening in her mind. "And, James is so sweet and encouraging … He really, really is. He picked me up a seashell." She held it up for Jacq to see it.

"It is lovely," she said, admiring the shell as best as she could in the poor lighting.

"Aye." She turned it over dreamily in her gloved hands before continuing. "And then I told him I did not think myself worthy of his devotion."

"What?" Jacq barely caught her voice level from spiking as she sat up and stared down at Alex. "Don't be ridiculous!"

"Well, it was how I felt," she returned. Her brow furrowed. "Now ssh! We do not need you waking Amy …" Glaring at her, Jacq granted her sister's request and settled back down in the blankets. "Where was I?" She thought a moment while Jacq got comfortable again. "Oh, yes … Well, when I said that, James took me by the hand and told me there was no other lass he would rather share his love with." She sighed distractedly. "And then … he asked me to marry him …"

Her eyes growing at this, Jacq found she was nearly speechless. "Wow … That's … That's …" She fumbled for words but stopped suddenly. "Well, wait, what'd you say?"

Turning a self-conscious gaze to Jacq, Alex then looked down at the seashell in her hand. "I kissed him."

"What?" Jacq sat upright again.

"I know … I do not know what came over me!"

194

"Well, never mind that! What'd he say?" Jacq scooted closer, whispering her question.

"He simply asked if it was a yes. I felt so foolish, though! How embarrassing and completely unladylike of me! I mean, really...What was I thinking?" Turning her face down into her pillow, a moment, not realizing how embarrassing it was until she was now telling Jacq.

"Well..." Jacq scratched her head. "What'd you say?"

Rolling out of burying her face, Alex grinned sheepishly. "I said yes!"

Shaking her head and grinning at her sister's antics, Jacq took a short glance at the window, which let in the moonlight. "I'm sure he'll be perfect for you..."

"You think so?" she asked timidly, obviously made shier by the telling of her little tale.

"Aye...And if he gets out of line, he'll have me to answer to..."

Giggling, Alex sat up and gave Jacq a small shove. "I am glad to have you as my sister. I cannot imagine never knowing you."

Smiling at this little confession, Jacq leaned over and embraced her. "I'm glad to know you too." *And as irony would have it,* she thought to herself, *we have Miata to thank for that...*

Chapter 13

"But it was all a lie!" Amy sobbed, racking her entire body as she clung to the cold, iron bars.

"I still raised you, child," Margaret reminded in her gentlest voice possible. "I apologize for the pain I have caused you these past few months. I did not intend any of it to take place as it did."

Silence crept in amongst the few who stood in the room, staring at the redhead behind bars. Margaret reached out to touch the hand of the girl, but she found her restraints would not allow her to stretch that far.

"How could you," Amy asked in a whimper, "intentionally deceive my father...our father...and I for this long and not feel guilt for it?"

"Whoever said I did not feel guilt?" Margaret sighed dejectedly.

Jacq's eyebrow rose at this; she threw a glance at Alex. Shaking her head, Alex gestured for her to wait.

"Guilt was on my mind every day," Margaret said, her voice becoming high-pitched. "Haha!" Her laugh sounded insane. "As a matter of fact, I swore I would do almost anything to fix what I had done if the chance arose."

Rolling her eyes, Jacq turned her back; Alex pinched her arm. Glaring, the twin turned back around to face the prisoner.

"Your account makes little sense." Amy sniffed through her tears. "You send my sisters away, separating them and not telling our father they exist. Then you carry on as my governess my entire life when *all* you desire is my father's hand in marriage...? I know not what to do with you," Amy said, her eyes narrowing into glaring slants.

"Why not let the court decide?" Pierce, who was still wearing tamer, more civilized attire as he was the night before, surprised everyone by suggesting. All eyes turned to him. Glancing between those present, he cleared his throat and carried on, "I am acquainted with Justice of the Peace Sir Walter Fleming. I could probably get us an audience with him today."

Nodding, Captain Turner stepped forward. "This is a fair idea. However, as the innocent party, you, Miss Amy, would be bringing the charges. You would have to choose this."

Jacq and Alex exchanged glances then looked over at Amy. Biting her lower lip, Amy cast a glance towards the older girls, seeking some sort of notion from them. Jacq bowed her head in support of the curly-haired blonde's decision. Alex also relinquished her input with the same gesture. Turning her gaze to Miata, who gave no signal on the matter, save a small, supportive smile on her behalf, she heaved a sigh. Twirling a lock of hair around her fingers as she contemplated, she was quiet for several seconds

before she finally lifted her gaze to look those awaiting her decision in the eye and spoke, "Very well. If Geoffrey Pierce can get an audience with the court, we will see the judge this very day. If the Justice of the Peace finds you to be guilty," she turned her attention to Margaret, "may you remain in a cell such as this for twice the number of years you deceived my family, or the rest of your natural life."

Margaret gasped. "Amy. You would do this to me? Throw away my very life?"

"Leaving me with the pirates wasn't throwing away mine?" Amy asked heatedly.

The redhead's mouth clamped shut, and she ran her hands over her hair as though trying to smooth it.

"I will go see if Sir Fleming can give us an audience. Permit me a short while to return," Pierce requested, gathering his things.

"Shall I accompany you, sir?" Mr. Bibbs asked.

"Nay, good man. Stay here in case something comes up. If there is a change of plans before I return, come for me immediately."

Mr. Bibbs eyed him pensively. "Of course, sir..." With that, Pierce vanished out the door, leaving everyone watching after him a little befuddled but slightly impressed.

Much to everyone's continued surprise, Pierce showed up about an hour later with news. "Well, I had to pull some strings," at this comment, Bibbs turned an eyebrow arched look to him, "but we have an audience with the

court this afternoon. We should go there now so when he is ready to see us, we will be there."

"That's wonderful," Amy spoke up, getting up from where she'd seated herself between Miata and Jacq. "I, for one, will be glad to have this unpleasant chore behind me."

The twins, sitting side by side, rose behind her. "Aye," Jacq stated. "I too will be glad to see this through." Alex looped her arm around her sister's.

At this, the rest of the company—Turner, Rackham, Monroe, and Miata hauled themselves to their feet. Releasing Margaret into the custody of the captain, the group then marched to the courthouse. As they marched along, Bibbs slowed his pace, catching Pierce's arm as he did so, allowing everyone else in the company to pass them. Once they were straggling behind, Mr. Bibbs cleared his throat and inquired, "Sir…You say we are going to have an audience with Sir Walter Fleming, friend of Governor Hobart, friend of, God rest his soul, your father?" Pierce sighed and tried to hasten his pace, but Bibbs caught him before he could catch up to the rest. "I just want to know why, sir…"

"I see goodness in her, Bibbs," he said. "Maybe I'm being a fool, but if I see it, I should do something about it, right?"

Looking away, Bibbs rubbed the back of his neck and sighed. "I suppose that is something you must determine for yourself, sir. I just hope, for your sake, that you are not disappointed with the outcome."

"If I am," Pierce huffed, "it will probably serve me right…"

They exchanged a glance of the sort they had never exchanged before—a glance of understanding. *He's finally growing up*, Bibbs thought, a smile breaking forth onto his face from within. Clapping him on the back, Bibbs chuckled, and they quickened their pace to catch up with the others.

When they arrived at the courthouse, they were not entirely surprised to see it was a relatively small building—reasonably well maintained but rather old. Opening the door for them, Mr. Bibbs held it as the caravan filed into the structure. As Jacq, bringing up the rear, passed him, he followed her in, closing the door behind them. As everyone seated themselves in the waiting area, of which was loosely strewn with a few farmers and fishermen, Bibbs wandered past Margaret and paused briefly, leaning down and saying in a hushed tone, "If you are released today, know that it is undoubtedly thanks to Mister Pierce." Breathing in a gasp of air, she turned her big green eyes, all jumpy and paranoid, up to stare at him. However, he walked away, hands behind his back, before she could comment on or question his statement.

After they were all present and seated, Pierce crossed over to where the court secretary and the court herald sat near the closed doors of the courtroom. "Please inform his honor, Sir Walter Fleming, that Miss Amy Luray and the accused Miss Margaret McLoflin are now present at his convenience."

"Of course, Mister Pierce," the court secretary, a plump fellow with a wide collar about his neck, said. Picking up his quill, he scrawled the names in his book. Then, turning to the herald, a far thinner man, he gestured him away to deliver the message to the judge.

Nodding his thanks, Pierce returned to sit with the group. Several moments ticked on. They watched the herald return, a very upset woman leave the courtroom, two farmers enter, and a few moments later leave looking neutrally content about their time spent on the other side of the heavy doors. Jacq leaned back where she sat and closed her eyes, thinking that perhaps sleeping might make the time go faster. As she relaxed, however, her brain began to question, *Pierce has been acting awful strange the last few days... Or is it actually normal? I wonder how difficult it was for him to get an audience for us today on such short notice...?* Sitting up at this, she opened her mouth to inquire about her curiosities, but as she did so, the doors opened, and the fisherman who'd gone in after the farmers came out, left in a seemingly upbeat mood.

Then, the herald rose from his place and gestured to the group. "Sir Walter Fleming!" At this, Pierce got up, motioning for everyone else to follow. "I present to you a civil case between Miss Amy Luray and the accused, Miss Margaret McLoflin."

"They may enter!" an old voice called back from the recesses of the courtroom.

The group entered, and Amy and Margaret were escorted to the front of the room while everyone else was directed to seating elsewhere in the room. Pierce and Mr. Bibbs—out of obligation—sat on the side behind Margaret, but everyone else set themselves down in a long row behind Amy. After everyone was stationary, the judge, a grand man with an old and tired demeanor hit his gavel on his podium

to summon silence. An apprehensive still came over the room, and he cleared his throat. "I, Justice of the Peace, Sir Walter Fleming declare this court, the Court of Port de Couler de Bateaux to now be in session, presiding over a civil case by Miss Amy Luray against the accused, Miss Margaret McLolflin." Jacq clutched Alex's hand.

He turned his dull, droopy eyes to Amy first. "Miss Amy Luray, correct?"

"Aye, sir!" she called out timidly.

"And," he looked at Margaret, "the accused, Miss Margaret McLoflin, correct?"

"Yes, sir," Margaret admitted.

"Miss Luray," the judge said, moving back to her, "state your case against Miss McLoflin."

"Your honor," Amy said, "Miss Margaret McLoflin has just been discovered to have sold off my sisters upon their mother's death, unbeknownst to my father. She has deceived my family for the last eighteen years, and on behalf of myself and others injured in these transgressions, I seek amends."

Jacq sat back, relaxing her hold on Alex. "She speaks mighty well…"

"You could too, if you wanted," Alex said, smiling over at Jacq. The twin rolled her eyes.

"And what have you to say to these charges?" the judge asked, going now to Margaret.

Taking a small step forward, Margaret held her hands out in pleading manner and addressed the judge with a teary glisten in her eyes. "Your honor, I admit to making a poor choice 18 years ago. However, I did not mean any harm to befall anyone! What I did was a blind and foolish act of love. I beseech you, your honor. My crimes are old, and to atone for them, I served as a governess for Miss Luray for the last sixteen years."

"Is this true?" Sir Fleming asked, turning again to Amy.

"Well, Miss McLoflin has been my governess, but she told my father it was because she felt bad for the death of his wife and child, not because she gave away his twin daughters and was secretly hoping to marry him!" Amy's voice made no doubt of her protest.

"Has she been negligent in her duties to you or your family in her position of governess for the past sixteen years?" he asked stodgily.

Amy ground her teeth, the muscles in her neck visibly tensing. "Other than keeping secrets from us, no; she has serviced our family well as my governess." An uncomfortable silence filled the room. Jacq watched Amy closely as the younger girl turned to look at them. The half sisters locked their stare a moment before Amy took a deep breath and returned her attention to the judge. "But, that does not clear her of the fact she gave away my sisters!"

Going back to Margaret, he cleared his throat. "And what have you to say to this, Miss McLoflin?"

"In my defense, your honor, I had not heard from Mister Luray for some time when I put the two girls up for adoption. I tried to get them adopted out together, but there is only so much control I had over that! When Mister Luray returned alive, it was difficult enough telling him of his wife's passing. I could not bear to tell him his daughters had been adopted out as well!"

"Surely they had family they could have been given to!" the judge returned, drumming his thick fingers in front of him.

"My lord," Margaret continued, "looking back, it was certainly not the best decision that I made, and for that I am sincerely apologetic. But, you must believe me when I say I did the best I could at that time!"

Jacq and Alex exchanged scowls. Miata, wringing his hands mercilessly, was watching the twins and Amy nervously. Turner, Monroe, and Rackham were nearly motionless, but their gazes were intense and fastened primarily on Sir Fleming. Pierce, on the other hand, seemed fairly relaxed, leaning back slightly in his seat beside Mr. Bibbs whose back was stiffly upright.

The judge was silent for several moments at this. A dreary, heavy silence that seemed to drag on three or four times longer than it really was. He looked between the faces scattered throughout the courtroom, all staring at him, pleading to see their side. He stared for a few moments at Amy, whose eyes were fretful and jumpy though she kept her exterior calm and collected. Then he looked over Margaret, who seemed jittery and anxious but had a mature, doleful silence that kept her mostly still except for an occasional tremble. Jacq began wiggling in her seat, and Alex found even she was restlessly shifting her weight.

Then, the older man cleared his throat, catching everyone's attention. Taking a glance at Pierce, he said in a belabored voice, "After considering the facts, I, Sir Walter Fleming, Justice of the Peace in the Court of Port de Couler de Bateaux, find the accused Miss Margaret

McLoflin to be guilty of perjury and issue a fine to her in the amount of one hundred shillings." Everyone, except Pierce, squirmed at this. "If the accused is unable to pay the fine stated, the accused will remain in custody for one full calendar year." Again, there was squirming.

"This is outrageous!" Jacq whispered to Alex. "Only a year?"

Alex's mouth dipped at the corner, and she shrugged. "There is nothing we can do."

"However," the judge continued saying, "the court has it in writing that the Pierce family will pay any fines of injustices found against the accused Miss Margaret McLoflin"—everyone started at this, except Pierce and Bibbs, and turned to stare at Geoffrey Pierce—"and will subsequently be paying one hundred shillings on behalf of Miss Margaret McLoflin to Miss Amy Luray and her family."

Jacq moved to rise in protest, but Alex and Miata caught her before she could get to her feet. Frowning, the judge picked up the gavel and dropped it three times. Each time the hammer fell, the deafening sound rang in Jacq's head and hit her chest like the punch of a large fist. "Case dismissed. Miss Margaret McLoflin, you are free to go as soon as the Pierce family covers your fine. Miss Amy Luray, you may collect the sum of your amends from the court secretary once the Pierce family has paid."

The room went silent. A silence so empty it was as if time had paused a moment. Jacq gaped at the judge as he rose from his seat behind the podium and walked through a small door in the back wall off to his left. Up front, Margaret returned to the grand stature she had acquired

while playing the part of Madam McLoflin, a high society woman with a thin, pointy nose and flaming red hair. Alex barely caught Jacq to stop her from lunging after the judge as Jacq fought the deep desire to bark out some uncouth remark. As the door Sir Fleming left through swung shut, Jacq stopped struggling, the truth sinking in. Her head bowed, her arms hanging at her sides, the decorative coins strewn about her attire still, she embodied defeat.

Touching Jacq's arm, Alex said in a tone hardly above a whisper, "Come. We should leave this place." Heaving a sigh, Jacq nodded. As the girls rose and the group followed, there was an undeniable feeling of awkward tension that stood with them. The twins and Miata eyed Pierce sharply, and he, though obviously uncomfortable, clenched his jaw and put on a tight-lipped smile. Amy and Margaret twisted edgily to come face to face with each other. Alex's lip began to tremble and, seeing this, Jim stepped forward and wordlessly put his arm about her shoulders. Dante, watching Jacq force herself forward, rubbed the back of his neck and cast a troubled glance to Captain Turner, who shook his head and patted the boatswain on the back.

At the front of the room, Amy and Margaret were still facing each other. "Well, congratulations. It seems fortune was on your side today," Amy said.

"Perhaps," McLoflin replied. "Although it seems like you are in good fortune yourself…"

Turning her head to observe the twins and Miata, who were shifting their feet as they stood across from Pierce, who seemed so still that he was potentially holding his breath, she let out a long exhale. "Perhaps … But it seems like there is someone who is quite fond of you …"

Margaret followed her gaze to Pierce. "Yes … Maybe I should give him a chance."

"It's possible it will be one of the best choices you'll have made in your life," Amy replied spitefully. Her eyes narrowing as she returned her look to Margaret. The redhead frowned, but held her tongue.

Back with the main group, Jacq, grinding her teeth, took a step toward Pierce and asked, "Why? Why did you do this?"

"I know you feel injured by this, but I had to. I can't explain it. I just had to," he said. His voice suggested he was conflicted, but that he had made his decision and was going to stick with it. "At least this way you can put these things behind you."

Her jaw tensing at this, she glared at him a moment then threw her gaze to the floor. *How dare he? Decide on his own if she is guilty or not …* At this thought, she stopped, her brow furrowing. *What am I saying? This is foolishness,* Jacq chided herself internally. *Who am I to condemn one for their foul deeds when I have done foul deeds myself?* Raising her eyes, she forced a mild smile onto her face. "Well, each of us must do what we believe to be right …"

As she spoke, Margaret and Amy came up to the rest of the group. At their presence, Pierce turned his attention to them. "It seems I have you to thank for part of my fortune," Margaret spoke in his direction, her manner far less proud than it had been in all of their previous attempts at discourse.

"I thought you deserved a second chance," he replied simply. "I did what I could to give you that."

Timidly, she drew a little closer to him and asked, "Might I join you for a short walk?"

Maintaining his cool front, though one could see hopeful bursts budding beneath his skin, he said, "Of course ... As soon as I speak with the court secretary ..." Holding out his arm, which she delicately threaded hers into, he then escorted her from the courtroom.

For a few minutes, everyone else gawked amongst themselves and fidgeted on their feet as they tried to absorb what all had just happened. After a short while had passed, Mr. Bibbs took the lead, saying, "Well, chaps, let us head out. There's nothing else for us here ..." Putting his hand on Jacq's shoulder, he led her out into the town streets, followed shortly by James and Alex, Miata and Amy—who stopped by the court secretary on her way out, and Captain Turner and Dante Rackham. The group, somewhat spread out, trudged down the street with slow, heavy steps.

The following morning, after a somewhat dreary evening, the group was cluttering the dock; the *Sea Dragon*, being loaded with its final provisions, was ready to set sail. Captain Turner said his good-byes to those staying behind first. When he came to the twins, he smiled gently. "I pray I have taught you as much as you have taught me. You lasses will find your father, of that I have no doubt." Moving to Jacq, he said, "And if you ever wish to sail aboard my ship as part of the crew, Miss Jacqueline, you shall be the first lady to do so." Tipping his hat, he turned; hands clasped behind his back, he marched up the ramp to the ship.

Waving, the sailors who weren't already aboard began to file onto the ship. Amy, Miata, Alex, Jacq, and Mr. Bibbs returned the gestures, smiling at the men they had come to know so well in the time they had spent together abroad. One of the cabin boys sidled up to Jacq and said, "Thank ye fer everythin', Miss Jacqueline!"

Kneeling to be level with the boy, Jacq smiled softly and asked, "What are you thanking me for?"

"Fer teachin' Skippy a thing o' two aboot cabin boys!"

Swatting him, Dante grinned sheepishly at Jacq. Her eyebrows rose in question to verify what the boy said as he scampered aboard and she returned to an upright stance. Shrugging, Dante casually said, "I wasn't that bad..."

As the last few men plodded onto the ship, Jim sighed and turned to face Alex. Holding her chin in his hand, he let his eyes absorb the image of her pretty face. A serene silence fell about those left on the landing dock. Jim's sky-blue eyes reflected her beautiful smile as she forced it onto her face. How long would it be until she saw him again? Holding her breath, Alex thought, *I told myself I would not cry.*

She is going to cry, Jacq thought, heaving a sigh as she watched them.

Biting her lip, Alex clenched Jim's fingers as he began to sorrowfully pull his hand away. *Don't...* she begged inside. *Don't... don't do it...*

209

Five…four…three… Jacq held out her arms, though Alex's back was still turned. Slipping his hand free, Jim forced himself to board the ship.

Flinging herself around, Alex fell into Jacq's open arms, hugging her more tightly than she had ever done before. Tears sprang from her eyes and raced each other down her face. As she began to catch her breath and calm, Alex said between sniffles, "This could be the end, Jacq."

"What?" Jacq asked, holding her sister at arm's distance so she could look her in the eye. "Stop such talk! You never know the end until you arrive, and then it matters not what the end shall be because you are there."

"And that is supposed to make me feel better?" Alex asked, trying not to blubber.

Pulling her back into an embrace, Jacq told her as she smoothed her hair, "Aye, lass. For you see, there is nothing to fear if you believe it will all be as it should."

Alex sniffled, tightening her grip on Jacq. "Forgive me my despair!"

Pulling partially away again, Jacq tilted her sister's face to meet her eyes and said, "Stop this nonsense. Count not your despair. Remember, sometimes angels fall…" Nodding, Alex smiled despite her desolation.

Looking Jacq up and down, Dante fidgeted for a moment, then stuck out his hand as an offer at good-bye. Glancing at her sister, who was sheepishly backing away and dabbing her eyes, Jacq reached for his hand. Just before she got hold of it, however, he guiltily let it drop. Pausing awkwardly, Jacq smiled and withdrew hers as well, searching his eyes for some sort of signal. Taking a step forward, the tall young man smiled and gently wrapped his arms about her. Eagerly, she returned the embrace, hoping it meant something good.

"I shall meet you here, Jacq, if you've a mind, to see the zebras," he whispered into her ear as he released her.

"Aye, mate." He soaked up her image as he straightened to his full height. "May the days pass swiftly and the winds fill your sails."

Giving her one last smile, he turned and gave Alex, Amy, and Miata a small nod before about facing and trudging up the ramp to the deck. As the ramp was drawn back, the crew waved their hands at the girls before scattering to their duties. The sun came out from hiding behind the early morning clouds, as beautiful as though it were June. Yet, as it shone gladly on those beneath it, drizzly rain began to fall from the sky, causing many of those standing at the dock to wander away and attend to their own business.

Smiling as she watched the *Sea Dragon* set sail, Jacq brushed both the tears rolling from her eyes and falling from the sky off her cheek. Reaching down to find her sister's hand, Alex glanced over at the bottle of mixed emotion she was standing beside. Quite suddenly, however, she noticed that arched over the ship was the most vivid rainbow she had ever seen. Tugging on the hand she was grasping and getting Jacq's attention, she pointed and said, "Look what you have done..."

Laughing halfheartedly, Jacq shrugged. "It's beautiful..." Quietly, she allowed her eyes to fall back to the shrinking ship ahead of them. "May the good LORD grant them swift passage..." Then, taking a deep breath, she

sang in a soft voice that only Alex could hear until it faded
with the ship:

So merry, so merry, so merry are we,
No matter who's laughing at sailors at sea.
Oh, hi derry, hey derry, ho derry down,
Give sailors their grog and there's nothing goes wrong,
I is the irons where the stuns'l boom sits,
J is the jib-boom that often does dip,
K are the keelsons of which you've told, and
L are the lanyards that always will hold.
So merry, so merry, so merry are we,
No matter who's laughing at sailors at sea.
Oh, hi derry, hey derry, ho derry down,
Give sailors their grog and there's nothing goes wrong,
M is the main mast, so stout and so strong,
N is the north point that never points wrong,
O are the orders of which we must be'ware, and
P are the pumps that cause sailors to swear.
So merry, so merry, so merry are we,
No matter who's laughing at sailors at sea…